MW00680860

The
Richest Person
in the World

Stan Toler

dustjacket

THE RICHEST PERSON IN THE WORLD
Copyright © 2011 by Stan Toler

ISBN: 978-0-9832729-7-7

Dust Jacket Press
PO Box 721243
Oklahoma City, OK 73172

www.DustJacket.com
Info@DustJacket.com

The characters and events in this book are fictional, and any resemblance to actual persons or events is coincidental.

Chapter One

"Where are you, Keith Richardson? And don't even try to tell me you're at work because I know better! They said you showed up today long enough to take a week's vacation. I've been leaving messages on your cell for hours."

Keith grimaced and held the phone away from his ear.

"Do you know how worried I've been? I was on the verge of calling the police. And now you answer like everything is business as usual—and *that* after I left *twelve messages!*"

His fingers tightened against the phone. Jenny's voice always screeched when she was mad. Today was worse than ever. He was certain his wife would take it up an octave if she knew he was in a taxi in Seattle. He'd stormed out this morning after their fight-of-the-day and never bothered telling her he'd hopped on a plane.

"Keith! Are you going to answer me?" she shrieked.

He envisioned his wife's reddened face, her intense brown eyes. The image left him indifferent for once. Keith couldn't even conjure the passion to return her anger.

"I'm in Seattle," he stated as if he were reciting the weather forecast. "I turned off my cell when I got on the plane. I'm okay," he added, "and by myself, for whatever that's worth." Without further explanation, Keith disconnected the call.

He'd added the bit about being by himself to hopefully circumvent another type of argument. Even though Keith had never been unfaithful, Jenny had put them both through misery with her jealousy. The last year had been worse than ever. Granted, a few women over the years *had* thrown themselves at him, despite his wedding band. But Keith had enough sense to keep his head and his wedding vows.

Too bad I haven't had that much sense elsewhere, he thought and winced against the 3:00 sunshine blasting through the cab's window like a heavenly spotlight. The cloudless skies and cool spring air couldn't have been more annoying. Even the Seattle rain was letting him down today. Keith would have preferred a gloomy, wet afternoon over this cheerful irritation.

Gritting his teeth, he loosened his tie and released his shirt's top button. The cab was as stuffy as the driver was blunt. The smell of stale cigars increased Keith's longing for fresh air. He was on the verge of shrugging out of his stifling overcoat when he leaned forward and strained for the first glimpse of Mac's Place. Once he spotted the green sign above the matching canopy, Keith's jaw relaxed. He was certain heaven's pearly gates were topped by a green canopy.

He closed his eyes and relaxed against the seat. The taxi's hum, the whirr and honking of traffic all blended with fond memories of a haven where he was accepted and appreciated for who he was. He couldn't remember the last time he'd seen that glow in Jenny's eyes. He wondered if he'd ever see it again.

His cell phone bleeped anew, and the distinctive ring indicated the caller was Jenny. Frowning, Keith glared at the phone he still held. The message icon validated Jenny's claim of leaving messages. The taxi slowed. Keith glanced out the window. Mac's Place was only feet away.

"That'll be $28," the driver barked and shot a glance toward Keith's noisy cell.

Keith pressed a button that ended the beeping and turned off the phone. He was in the mood for coffee and nothing else. He dropped the phone into his overcoat pocket, dug out his billfold, flipped the driver his fee and tip, grabbed his briefcase, and emerged into the sunshine.

The second the taxi door banged shut behind him, Keith was amazed at how a place so familiar could appear so new after only a few years. He gazed at the storefront of the small café and coffee shop, once his primary hangout. The place hadn't changed much. Yet he had changed in ways he couldn't explain, and the new Keith longed to connect with the man he once had been—the man who'd claimed Mac's Place as his second home.

The only thing that would have made the moment perfect was a sudden downpour that would force Keith to pull his coat over his head and make a mad dash for the door. *It was pouring the last time I left Mac's Place*, he reflected and glanced toward the sky. Any hopes of rain were annihilated. The sky was as cloudless as when the plane landed. Unable to stand the overcoat another second, Keith slipped his billfold into his pants pocket, shrugged out of the coat, and draped it over his arm.

A breeze danced along the street and cooled the perspiration beading his collar. The cold moisture brought back even more memories. Three years ago when Keith left Seattle, he had been lighthearted in spite of the downpour that soaked him to the skin. He would never forget his last night in his favorite coffee shop. The visit had turned into a celebration of his new job and new wife. Today he felt as if both had turned into boulders he was dragging uphill.

As he stepped forward, the cell phone in his coat pocket bumped against his thigh. A hint of guilt nibbled at the back of Keith's mind, but he dashed it away. His bankrupt life needed change. And the relationship with Jenny was at the top of the list. As long as Keith continued to interact on the old levels, the relationship would remained stagnant. Of course, hanging up on her and turning off his cell weren't exactly the steps toward a fresh start either.

The cafe's door opened. The smell of creamy cappuccino and the house's special mellow brew enveloped him in a welcoming beckon. A stocky man exiting looked Keith squarely in the face and didn't even smile. Keith returned the favor.

While impatient pedestrians maneuvered around him, Keith took several hesitant steps toward the door. *What if no one remembers me?* he worried. *And Joe? What about Joe? What if he's not even here anymore?*

He reached for the worn, brass knob…and then pulled back.

What if they do *remember me and ask how I'm doing?* Somehow, in his drive to escape his problems, Keith had failed to assess the dynamics of his old haven. In longing for the comfort of the past, he'd neglected to prepare himself if they'd forgotten him—or practice his speech if they remembered him.

The door opened again. This time a young woman exited. She was about 30, had long blonde hair, and the kind of eyes a man remembered. When she took a second look at Keith, he thought of Jenny and ignored her.

He was here to remember…to be remembered, and nothing more.

Laughter greeted Keith as he slowly turned the knob and pushed open the beveled glass door. The sweet smell of blended coffee beans wafted over him like a warm blanket. Keith absorbed the ambiance of worn, wooden floors and the antique service bar that welcomed him home. He spotted a small group of men sitting at a table near the counter and recognized the guy at the center of attention: Joe, as usual. And the best Keith could tell the guy was about to win the corniest-joke-of-the-century award again. He smiled, increased his pace, and relished the sound of creaking floorboards. The closer he grew to the group the more his problems faded.

"So the panda gets up and heads toward the door," Joe said, his back to Keith.

Keith noted his friend wore the usual gear—a pair of jeans and a long-sleeved T-shirt with *Mac's Place* scrawled across the back.

"And the waiter said, 'Hey, you can't come into my restaurant and act like that,'" Joe continued midst the low chuckles rippling through the group. "So the panda says, 'I'm a panda, pal. This is my regular routine. Look it up in the dictionary.'"

Joe paused before delivering the next line. "So the waiter walked over to the bookshelf, grabbed a dictionary, and read—"

"'Panda. Native of China,'" Keith interrupted. "'Eats, shoots, and leaves!'"

The tiny audience turned inquisitive stares toward him. One began a hesitant snicker, and then another, until everyone at the table was laughing at the stolen punch line.

Everyone, that is, except Joe. The former basketball player stood to his towering height and turned to face his joke spoiler.

"Keith Richardson!" he accused with a broad grin that revealed his chipped front tooth. "Of all the coffee joints in the world, you had to walk into mine! And I was on a roll!"

"Joseph Conrad, you never could tell that joke right. Good thing I got here when I did." Keith dropped his briefcase and over-coat into an empty chair.

A quick handshake turned into a back-whacking hug.

"What has it been? Three years?" Joe stepped back, gripped Keith's shoulders, and looked his friend eye to eye.

"Three years, one month, ten days. But who's counting?" Keith tried to sound upbeat, but he wasn't sure he'd even come close to fooling Joe. His keen eyes missed little. Keith averted his gaze, and spotted a cup of steaming coffee that called his name.

"Seems like yesterday we were holding your farewell party," Joe recalled. "Hey, remember the skit Rick and Charlie did? Rick was playing you, trying to get onto an airplane carrying that guitar of yours and hitting everything and everyone in sight."

Keith smiled and continued the story. "Charlie played the female flight attendant, trying to get me to my seat without killing anyone. Of course we all nearly killed ourselves laughing at Charlie's scrawny legs sticking out of that skirt. That was quite a skit—and closer to the truth than they'll ever know. I still have that guitar, but I don't take it on airplanes anymore."

"Good!" A tall, bearded man from the next table stood and walked toward Keith. "But I'll have to say it's more dangerous when you're playing it than when you're swinging it at people."

"Oh, I don't know," replied a short, scrawny guy who made a

similar move. "I always thought his singing was more lethal than his guitar playing."

"Rick! Charlie! You two old coots! I didn't even *see* you!"

As usual the two regulars had blended with the scenery at Mac's Place like a well-worn bar stool that no one sees but everyone enjoys. The hand-pumping and back-whacking resumed, and Keith came close to convincing himself that the last three years had never happened. But the memories of the morning's bitter fight and his credit card being declined at the airport insisted that the last three years had happened, and happened with a vengeance.

"When did they let you two out of jail?" Keith chided with a sarcastic grin.

"They threw 'em out!" Joe chimed in. "The other inmates complained that their horrible puns were cruel and unusual punishment."

"The jailers separated us," Rick spoke up. When he wiggled his brows, Keith noticed one of them had nearly been replaced by a mangled scar. "So we had to use 'cell' phones to talk to each other." He tugged on his graying beard, which was as pale as his skin was dark.

Keith's groan mingled with Charlie's.

"That was really bad, man," Charlie countered.

"See what I mean?" Joe said and rolled his eyes.

"Boy, it's good to see you clowns!" Keith couldn't have stopped his grin even if he tried. "I had no idea who might be here today." He gazed around the sparsely occupied tables but recognized no one else.

"What brings you to town?" Charlie asked as he pulled a couple of chairs up to their table. They all sat down except for Joe, who stopped by the joke victims for a quick word and then hustled behind the coffee bar.

"I flew in from Detroit for some *real* coffee," Keith replied and longingly gazed toward the stainless steel machines and coffee-related gadgets behind the service bar. Nobody could do coffee like Joe.

"Good choice!" Joe said with a wave. "I've always said my coffee's worth a trip across the nation."

"Oh brother!" Charlie complained. "He's having another ego attack."

"When you're good, you're good," Joe said with a bow fit for an encore.

Keith glanced toward his two companions.

"Makes me want to put salt water in the Bunn," Rick mumbled.

"What an idea," Charlie whispered. His blue eyes bulging with mirth, he nudged the saltshaker toward his friend.

The three shared a chuckle, and Keith was so inspired he removed his tie and suit coat and dropped them in the chair with his overcoat. Something about the "Vietnam vets turned fishermen" always made Keith want to slob out in a pair of frayed jeans and a leftover shirt and think about nothing but whether or not the cooler was full of Cokes and if there was still bait on his hook.

"What are you two up to now?" Joe eyed the pair and included Keith in his final glare.

"Who us? We wouldn't—"

"What makes you think we'd—"

The two continued with such innocent-sounding platitudes and guileless expressions that Keith laughed outright.

"If you run with those two long, *you'll* be in jail, Keith!" Joe warned with a fond grimace. Then, without missing a beat, he asked, "So what'll it be? You want a Red Eye?"

"You remembered!" Keith said. Joe's Red Eye—a shot of espresso in a cup of Mac's Blend—was the sweetest. "Can you add some cream?" he asked and stood.

"Cream! When did you pick up that nasty habit?"

"Up in Michigan." Keith meandered toward the service bar and settled onto his favorite bar stool. The fit was as good now as it had been three years ago. He relaxed against the back and nearly closed his eyes to savor the moment.

"I found me a coffee shop there," Keith continued, but he didn't add that the place was as personable as a sterilized surgery ward. "Problem is their coffee smelled like a pair of gym shoes after an all-day basketball tourney. I had to do something. Now I'm kind of used to it. You can leave it out if you want."

Joe smiled even broader. "For you, dear friend, I'll bring out the half & half." He went to the small refrigerator behind the bar, mixed the cream with the coffee and espresso, and handed the steaming cup of coffee to Keith.

He eagerly sipped the velvet liquid and savored the way it slipped down his throat and warmed his stomach. He inhaled the steam and went for another swallow before sliding off the stool and following Joe back to Rick and Charlie's table.

"Now tell us. What gives?" Joe grabbed his chair, turned it backward, straddled the chair, plopped into the seat, and rested his arm along the top rung. "Are you just visiting, or can we persuade you to give up your dreams and move back to Seattle?"

Keith strangled on his latest swallow and hacked until he reached his vacated chair.

"Look what you've done now," Rick accused. "You've gone and choked him up."

Laughing through the final coughs, Keith waved away Rick's claim. "I'm okay. You just surprised me, that's all. Do you really think I could come back home?" he asked, and the craving to resume his old life was as poignant as the coffee's smooth taste.

Joe looked across the table to his old friend, and then glanced back toward Rick and Charlie. "Whadda ya think, guys?" he asked.

"You got my vote," Rick said.

"Mine too!" Charlie added, his deeply lined lips curving into a wicked smile. "Maybe you could do something to stop Joe from going bald."

For the first time Keith noticed Joe's sandy red hair was thinner than he remembered.

Joe observed Charlie's balding head and drolly said, "Maybe you could, Keith. These guys don't have any answers, that's for sure."

"Hey, speak for yourself," Rick said and pulled at a handful of graying hair every bit as thick as his beard.

"You people are nuts!" Keith said and couldn't believe he'd forgotten just how zany this trio could get.

"It's unanimous then!" Joe exclaimed.

Still drowning in the sea of bald jokes, Keith didn't follow Joe's meaning. "What is?" he asked. "That you're nuts?"

"No!" Joe laughed outright. "Our vote on your coming home. I guess it all depends on whether or not you want to."

Keith's smile faded. He gazed into his coffee cup and wondered at the chances of Jenny's willingness to relocate. She had made a full-time job of decorating their lake house, and now she had the home just like she wanted it. Problem was, she didn't know they might have to sell the showplace just to be able to eat.

Standing, Keith walked toward the brick fireplace, smoldering with leftover coals and a few flickers. Joe used the ancient fireplace for atmosphere more than anything else. Most the heat went up the chimney even when it was needed for warmth. Although his hands weren't cold, Keith extended them toward the fire in hopes the chill in his heart might vanish. The result was toasty fingers and a heart that remained frigid. Feeling the gazes of his three friends, Keith slowly turned toward the table.

"I'm not the same person I was when I left," he told the wooden floors.

A klatch of customers exited the store. The door clunked shut.

"I'm not sure that you'd like the new Keith." He never took his attention from the floor. "I know I don't," he added, like a man who'd lost something but wasn't sure what. He examined the toes of his shiny wing tips and wondered why he'd let the salesman talk him into the $300 menaces. The silence that penetrated his mind was broken only by the soft mumble of the joke victims, the only other group now left in the shop.

Finally Keith looked up to see the three old friends eyeing one another. All jesting was over. Instead, Charlie and Rick communicated with a series of shrugs, raised brows, and pointed stares that insisted Joe say something. Keith always said those two could communicate more in a glance than most people said all day. Joe got to his feet and walked toward Keith.

"Whazzup, man?" he asked. He picked up the poker and nonchalantly stirred the dying embers.

Keith turned toward the fire. "I'm in debt up to my neck," he whispered and wondered why he ever imagined he'd need a speech with Joe. As usual he was free to tell all just like it was. "I'm one of the the top stockbrokers in my firm, but I'm still close to bankruptcy. I made a wrong move…or three…in the market a year ago, and I've barely been able to stay afloat ever since. On top of that, my marriage is coming apart at the seams. All Jenny and I do is fight."

"I guess the pressure's gotten to her too, then."

"No way. She doesn't know." Keith shook his head.

Joe's raised brows were as communicative as Charlie and Rick's ever were. "She doesn't know?"

"No." Keith hung his head, slipped his hands into his pockets, and nudged at the fireplace brick with the toe of his shoe. There were no words to explain what financial failure felt like—especially for a guy who was so good with other people's money. How he'd managed to mismanage his own was an irony that just wouldn't quit. Jenny had blindly trusted him, not only with their finances, but with her inheritance as well—$300,000. And now Keith's wrong decisions and her penchant for spending had sent them into a downward spiral he saw no way out of unless they sold their beloved home.

"Come on. Sit back down, why don't you?" Joe took Keith's arm and led him back to the table. "You're tired. And you're among friends here. Just sit and relax. You don't have to say another word if you don't want to."

"But I should," Keith said. Slumping into the empty chair, he caught the final stages of a Charlie–Rick silent enquiry. And Keith decided there was no need to hide the truth from these two guys. They were like two fond uncles who would be there for him no matter what.

"That's why I came here," Keith continued. "I took a week's vacation just to be with my friends—to see if I could figure out what's wrong with me and how all this happened." He curled his fingers around the chair's arms and dug his nails into the aged wood. In as few words as possible, he began relating the facts to Charlie and Rick and Joe. Finally, Keith loosened his grip and raised his hands to his eyes. When he lowered his fingers, they were moist. Oddly, Keith barely recognized his own emotion. Instead, he'd gone into the numb mode that had allowed him to function the last few months. Without the numbness, Keith was certain he would have gone stark raving mad ages ago.

"When I got laid off from my job here in Seattle," he continued, "you guys know I was offered that whopper of a job in Detroit. So I didn't have much choice but to move! No one was hiring here, and I figured I'd be crazy not to grab it fast. Everything was great until a year ago. I made several wrong moves in the stock market—took a chance or two I shouldn't have—and now I'm worse than broke. I'm on the verge of bankruptcy."

Keith picked up the saltshaker and examined the simple, stainless steel lid. "I've started avoiding Jenny and working overtime. But no matter how much I work, we never seem to have enough money. We can barely make ends meet." He set down the saltshaker and picked up his coffee mug. "And, well, things between Jenny and me aren't so good."

Taking a long swallow of his coffee, Keith wished his story was as comforting as the brew. He focused for a moment on a row of framed black-and-white photos lining the far wall. Many depicted the original owner, Mac, in his early days as a coffee shop owner.

"Right now all I want to do is escape. I'd rather die than have to tell my wife what a failure I am."

"So you came back to the ol' place for some answers and a good cup of coffee," Charlie said, breaking the dark cloud that hovered over the table.

"Yeah." Keith's attention rested on Charlie's gnarled hand curled around his own mug. His index finger was missing—so was his pinky. He eyed Charlie's denim shirt, as worn and scarred as its owner. Then he looked into Charlie's satisfied eyes. Keith would have given his whole hand for the peace he saw there.

Rick stroked his beard. "Sounds to me like the boy needs ICU. Whatcha think, Joe?"

"Absolutely." Joe nodded. "You two wantta watch the shop for me until Lila gets here?" He checked his wristwatch. "She's due in an hour."

"Sure thing." The two nodded, and Keith knew neither of them would really put saltwater in the coffee maker.

"Let's get you out to my place then." Joe stood and gripped Keith's shoulder. "Marcy will be so glad to see you, and it will give her somebody else to boss around besides me."

"But I planned to get a room at a hotel. And some time or other I need to make a stop at a department store. I didn't even pack for this trip. All I've got is what I'm wearing and my briefcase." He pointed toward the case sitting nearby.

"No problemo." Joe waved away all concerns. "I'll take care of everything. And Marcy wouldn't hear of you staying anywhere else." Joe stood, gathered the empty cups from the table, and walked back to the bar. "And if you try to argue, I'll lock you in a room with Rick and Charlie and let them tell you stupid puns all night!"

"Oh..." Charlie groaned.

"That was a low blow," Rick protested.

"Okay, you win! Anything but that!" Keith held up his hands in mock surrender as Charlie and Rick continued to protest the teasing.

Chapter Two

He's having an affair. He's having an affair. I just know he's having an affair. The mantra marched through Jenny Richardson's mind like a band of soldiers seizing territory. Her sight blurry from hours of crying, Jenny thumbed through a silver-plated album that held her and Keith's wedding photos.

When she got to the photo that included her mother, a fresh deluge of tears coursed where the others had dried. "Oh, Mom," she sobbed, "if only you were here! You'd know what to do." But Jenny's mother wasn't here. She hadn't been here for two years now. Jenny spent her teen years mourning the loss of her birth mother. Then, a decade later, she was faced with mourning the loss of her adoptive mother. Jenny was still stunned every time she thought of the beautiful-yet-zany sixty-year-old skydiving to her death when her parachute didn't open. Mom—always the daredevil nobody could stop.

Even though Jenny's sister knew their mom was taking skydiving lessons, neither she nor her mom had bothered telling Jenny—probably because they both knew Jenny would have a fit. Forever cautious, Jenny had been more like her father. Elaine, on the other hand, probably *encouraged* their mother to take up sky-diving. When Elaine called Jenny with news of their mom's death, her first reaction was anger. Their father had died of a massive heart attack five years before. Now Jenny was left with no parents, and she wasn't sure she was completely over the rejection from her birth mother even now. All that equaled more pain and loneliness than she ever wanted to endure.

She covered trembling lips with her fingers and focused on another photo that included Elaine and her husband, Allen. Elaine, her parents' biological daughter, was as dark and statuesque as Jenny was petite and blonde. She'd been Jenny's matron of honor, and Allen had been an usher. The two looked like they were posing for the cover photo of *Perfect Marriage Magazine.*

Fleetingly Jenny thought about calling her sister and begging for advice, but she dismissed the thought as quickly as it came. Elaine couldn't even come close to understanding Jenny's pain. Allen was such an attentive husband and father; he could be a candidate for the *Husband of the Year International Award.* In the last year Keith hadn't even come close to Allen's level of husbandly commitment.

"There's no way Elaine would know what to do," Jenny decided and lowered her feet to the plush carpet.

She snapped the album shut and gazed around the meticulously decorated home that she'd poured her soul into. Going for a classic appeal, Jenny had spent hours choosing exactly the right pieces to bring out the best in the home…from the brocade drapes to the velvet settee to the antique mantel that engulfed the fireplace like the gate of a fortress. She'd spent a small fortune on the decor, but the results were priceless. Keith had hosted party after party for his firm and even cut a few killer deals in the den. And Jenny had always been in the background, making certain the fine details were perfect—right down to the right potpourri that tinged the air with sweetness.

Now Keith had gone to Seattle with *her*...whoever she was. Jenny had become suspicious when he started spending more time at the office than at home. Now her heart confirmed her suspicions. Even his insistence he was alone enhanced the vision of a tryst with some floozy.

Jenny stood, slammed the wedding album against the sofa, and rubbed at the tears. Her puffy eyes burned and threatened more moisture. She gritted her teeth, curled her fists, and refused to give in to another tear.

After stomping into the kitchen, she whipped open the freezer door. The half gallon of chocolate almond ice cream was half gone. Last night it had been new. Jenny snatched up the carton, banged shut the freezer door, and yanked open the silverware drawer. She grabbed a spoon, rammed the drawer shut, and flipped the carton's lid into the sink. Glaring out the kitchen window, she shoveled a tablespoon of the nut-laden dessert into her mouth and couldn't conjure a trace of guilt for the indulgence.

Scrutinizing the backyard, she searched for even a hint of a lack of symmetry. She found none. Jenny had slavishly arranged for the complete relandscaping of the yard, right down to the bamboo strategically planted along the side of the property near the pool. After three years of waiting, the bamboo was coming up as predicted and lending the yard the Asian flair Jenny had envisioned. The evening sun christened the green shoots in a pale, golden frost that enhanced their image of health. Unfortunately, her three-year marriage wasn't showing nearly the growth of the bamboo. It was marriage dying in its infancy.

Jenny looked down at her size-five biking shorts and reminded herself she was supposed to be at the gym, but she didn't even care. The man she'd kept herself in shape for had barely noticed her for months, and he was now in the arms of another!

She crammed another chunk of cold confection into her mouth and chewed the almonds. After the fourth bite wove its cold path to her stomach, she drummed her sculptured nails against the marble-topped counter. Narrowing her eyes, Jenny made a decision. The time had come to consider the scary plan she'd shoved to the edge of her mind. While it was as methodical as the one she'd used when landscaping the yard, this scheme was much more risky—nearly like relationship skydiving. And if her parachute didn't work, her marriage could crash to its death.

The spoon trembled in her hand. For the first time, Jenny allowed that plan to begin a slow rotation through her mind. Her knees quivered. She didn't need to consult Elaine or even her best friend, Rochelle. Jenny *knew* what she had to do. But whether or not she'd have the courage to pull it off was another thing altogether.

Keith jolted and sat straight up into the darkness…into a swirl of jumbled thoughts. He strained to see through the unfamiliar shadows as a sense of panic seized his soul. He swung his feet to the floor, stood, and fought the urge to blindly run. Keith pressed his fists against his temples and tried to remember where he was and why he was there.

The fight with Jenny crashed through his thoughts. The plane ride to Seattle. The trip to Mac's Place. Joe and Charlie and Rick. Marcy…she'd welcomed him with open arms. She'd taken one look at him and insisted he go upstairs and lie down for a short rest before dinner.

"Dinner!" Keith whispered and rubbed his face. His stomach rumbled. He swiveled to eye the digital clock sitting on the nightstand. Four-thirty blared back at him. *How can it be so dark at 4:30?* he wondered and gazed toward the curtains covering the farmhouse's window. A security light's gentle glow oozed around the curtains, lending the ghost-like shadows an ethereal aura.

He frowned against the pasty taste in his mouth and recalled that he hadn't lain down until 4:30. Keith stumbled to the window and yanked aside the curtains. The sky was as dark as his soul felt. He rubbed the front of his rumpled shirt and wiggled his toes in his socks.

I can't believe I slept so long! Keith tried to remember the last time he'd slept more than three hours straight all night and couldn't. When his body sank onto that bed in the loft room last night, he'd felt like he hadn't slept in years.

Keith fumbled his way back to the bed and clicked on the nightstand lamp. The gauzy glow illuminated the room's rustic simplicity. He'd fallen in love with Joe and Marcy's log cabin the minute he saw it. The place was Marcy's folks old wheat farm and was located over an hour east of Seattle in Ellensburg. The cabin fit the acres surrounding it and appeared to have grown from the land it was sitting on. The inside was as simple and inviting as the outside.

The stark contrast between this place and his palatial home brought Jenny to the forefront of his mind. Keith's attention darted to his overcoat, draped across a padded rocker in the corner. Before crashing on the bed, he'd deleted all twelve of Jenny's agitated messages and then turned off the phone again.

With a combination of dread and expectation, he stepped toward the coat and pulled the phone from the folds. He pressed the on button and waited for the "Message Waiting" icon that would indicate the inevitable: more messages from his wife. But after staring at the phone a full thirty seconds, Keith realized there were no messages waiting. His brows flexed.

Odd, he thought and somehow missed what he'd dreaded.

His gaze wandered and Keith discovered a pair of jeans and a sweatshirt folded on the dresser. A note atop the clothing indicated these were for his use—along with a toothbrush and toiletries in a shaving bag beside the clothing. Yawning, Keith padded into the bathroom and prepared to shower.

By 5:00 Keith had also found a pair of work boots and socks with a sticky note on them that simply said "Keith." Surprisingly, the boots fit, if you didn't count the tad of wiggle room here and there. His stomach rumbled, and Keith decided he'd find the kitchen if it killed him. He'd barely eaten lunch yesterday, and Joe's cup of coffee at three was the last thing his stomach saw. He knew he was hungry when the bar of Ivory soap he bathed with looked delicious.

By the time he descended the steps, Keith realized he only had to follow his nose and the sounds of clanking dishes in order to find the kitchen...and that was a mere ten feet from the base of the stairs. Keith strode through the quaint living room and rounded the corner, into the odors of freshly cooked bacon, scrambled eggs, and coffee that smelled like it came straight from heaven.

Joe swiveled from the stove and quipped, "Hark! Who goes there?"

Keith chuckled. "What are *you* doing up so early?"

"Me? I'm up this time every morning. Marcy's been working the night shift at the hospital for weeks now. She'll be home soon. I've been in charge of having breakfast ready for us."

"Oh really?" Keith questioned. "Doesn't Marcy like to cook breakfast?"

"Sure. She enjoys cooking, but this is something I can do for her. A little spoiling goes a long way with wives, ya know." Joe winked.

Keith's gaze slid toward the coffeepot as he tried to remember the last time he'd cooked for Jenny. He came up with no time… ever. A fog of guilt threatened to consume him, but he recalled all those heated messages he'd deleted. The resulting irritation swept aside his guilt.

That woman could nag the shell off a turtle, he thought.

Keith didn't allow himself to admit that his skipping town without telling her was reason enough for her to be irate, let alone nag.

"I could use a gallon of that coffee," Keith said and stepped toward the pot. He conned himself into believing the hot liquid would wash away the memories of marital turmoil. "Man, I can't believe I slept so long," he mumbled as he reached for one of the mugs hanging from a hook under the cabinet.

"Right, but remember, it's eight o'clock back east," Joe said through a grin.

"Yeah, I thought about that in the shower…" Keith filled his mug and replaced the carafe, "…when I nearly ate the soap."

"That could be interesting." Joe widened his eyes and wiped his hand across the butcher's apron that featured a farmer pounding rocky soil. "Farmers Rock" was scrawled beneath the image. "I can just see bubbles coming out your ears or something."

Keith's growling stomach insisted he ignore the quip. "I'm starved," he said and considered burying his whole face in the mound of scrambled eggs sitting on the stove's center.

Joe picked up the platter and shoved it toward Keith. "Here." He pointed toward a drawer near the coffeepot. "The forks are in there. Eat all you want."

"You aren't going to eat any?"

"I wouldn't *dare*. You'd probably bite my arm off."

Chuckling, Keith balanced the mug and platter of eggs while retrieving a fork from the drawer. "When do you head for work?"

"Ah, my friend, ownership does have its privileges," Joe said, his gray eyes alight with confidence. "Since Marcy and I moved to Ellensburg, I've had to balance the farm with the shop. I have a one-room apartment in the back of the shop. I drive up Monday and stay through Tuesday evening." He reached for the carton of eggs sitting on the cabinet. "Then I come home and don't drive back in until Friday morning. I stay through Saturday night and then come back home. These are my usual days off anyway, but I called Lila last night." He cracked an egg, opened it over the grill, tossed the shell toward the sink, and grabbed another egg. "She's my new manager. Rick's niece, actually. She's agreed to take care of the place all week. That lady is a godsend."

"Sorry to upset your schedule," Keith apologized, "sort of," he added and eyed another platter. This one held crispy bacon and Belgian waffles the size of football stadiums. His mouth watered anew.

Joe piled the bacon and a choice waffle onto Keith's plate. "You *are* my schedule today. And tomorrow, and the day after if needed. You're like a brother to me." He gripped Keith's shoulder. "You arrived at my door a hurtin', and Dr. Joe's here to help you back to health." His broad smile revealed laugh lines that were deeper than Keith remembered. "First thing I need to tell ya, though, is that Ivory soap is hazardous to your health." Joe picked up a fork.

"Ah, man," Keith chided and set his plate and mug on the kitchen table, "all you doctors are the same. You always want us to quit all the fun stuff." He plopped into a high-backed chair and picked up a slice of bacon. Keith bit into the bacon, rolled his eyes, and nearly moaned as it slid down his throat. His stomach roared for more.

"Whether you want to hear it or not, all the latest studies show that bath soap is the most addictive substance out these days." Joe stopped scrambling the eggs and held up his fork. He grinned. "Substance abuse is substance abuse. It's got to stop."

Keith crammed a forkful of eggs into his mouth and chewed through a grin. "You're as big of a nut as you ever were."

Joe turned toward the refrigerator and retrieved a tub of butter. He whipped open a nearby cabinet and the syrup was next. "Here," he said and set the butter and syrup on the table. "I'll cook your waffle, but I won't butter and syrup it…or feed it to you either, for that matter."

"You won't have to." Keith snatched up the butter and swathed a thick layer on the waffle. He followed that with a river of syrup and started cutting the waffle. "I promise, if you weren't already married, I'd marry you myself."

"Okay, that's it!" Joe picked up the plate. "No more! You're getting *too weird.*"

"I've *been* weird." Keith snatched the plate from Joe and hunched his shoulders. Turning away, he shoved a mammoth bite of waffle into his mouth and looked over his shoulder toward his friend while he chewed.

Through a heartfelt laugh, Joe punched Keith's arm, then turned to the eggs. Once he had them safely on his plate, Joe moved toward the coffeepot. He picked up a mug near the stove and refilled it.

Keith placed his plate back on the table and consumed the rest of his meal. As his stomach filled, the momentary jesting passed away. The sizzle of more bacon echoed from a distant land, and his troubles clouded his thoughts.

I wish kicking an Ivory soap addiction was my only problem, he worried and didn't even think it was funny anymore.

"I don't even know how to start with what's wrong with me." Keith pushed aside his plate. He picked up the coffee mug and thought of Jenny…wondered if she was awake…wondered if she was thinking of him. He fingered the cell phone he'd slipped into his shirt pocket.

"You told me more than you know yesterday," Joe said as he settled into the chair across from Keith.

"What?" Keith blinked and focused on his friend, who was placing his breakfast plate on the table.

"You said you don't know how to start with what's wrong with you. But you've already told me more than you know." Joe shoveled a bite into his mouth.

"Oh. I didn't know you heard that."

"I'm the all-knowing ears of the kitchen. Nothing gets past me." Joe winked. "And yesterday at the coffeehouse, you were practically screaming your symptoms to all of us." He picked up the butter knife and gouged it into the yellow tub.

Keith eyed Joe's crisp waffle. It held no appeal. "Aren't you going to wait for Marcy?" he asked.

"Uh-uh," Joe said and lifted the butter-laden knife. "I'm good but not *that* good. Watching you eat was *too much*."

Keith laughed and rubbed his eyes. "And here I was thinking you were a way better husband than I am." He looked down and hesitated. "I've never cooked for Jenny."

"I'm long on cooking and short on waiting," Joe admitted, "especially when there's a brute eating in front of me."

Keith slid his friend a sour look. "I guess I'm short on everything," he grumbled. *Like money*, he added to himself. He narrowed his eyes and toyed with the brass napkin holder in the table's center.

"O.K., Doc," he said with more gusto than he felt, "tell me about my problems. What all did I reveal?"

"Aside from the Ivory soap issue…" Joe buttered the waffle as if he were smoothing the surface of freshly poured cement on a new patio. "Money problems out the ears. You and Jenny are on the verge of splitting. You're fighting like crazy. You're wearing yourself out, and at the end of the month, you still have more month left than money. I believe you're suffering from Financial Failure Syndrome." He looked up from his frosted waffle and lifted a brow. "How's my diagnosis?"

Keith stared into his coffee cup and recalled yesterday's conversation at Mac's Place. Joe didn't say anything that Keith didn't recall stating himself. But hearing the information from Joe gave Keith a better perspective. Nevertheless, the black liquid seemed as bottomless as his problems. He took a sip and barely nodded.

"Yeah," he admitted. "Financial Failure Syndrome pretty much sums it up. Got a chest full of gold you'll let me have?" He shot a tight smile toward his friend.

Joe chuckled and swallowed a bite of bacon. "No, but I can tell you how to get one."

"Yeah, right," Keith said.

"Okay, maybe not a *chest full*," Joe said, and thoughtfully shoved at his waffle. "But at least a tried-and-true way to stop sinking and start floating."

Keith lifted his gaze. His fingers flexed against the cup.

Joe laid down his fork and picked up his mug. "You know, there are several ways to acquire more money. You can work like a Turk, but you've already seen the problem with that. The harder you work, the further behind you get. You can inherit it or win it, but you know that can disappear just as quickly as it arrives."

"Tell me about it," Keith muttered.

"You can marry it."

"Been there. Done that. It's not looking good."

"Yes…and sometime you're going to *have* to tell Jenny about your finances."

Keith set down his mug and raised his hand. "I just keep thinking I'll somehow make a right move and get it back." He cradled his head in his hands and closed his eyes. "I just don't understand why I can make money for other people, but I keep hitting the pits with my own."

"Maybe it's not God's will for you to financially succeed right now."

Keith raised his head and stared at Joe. "What? Are you saying God is, like, *doing* this to me?"

"No, I think you did it to yourself."

"Thanks!" Keith gritted his teeth.

"I just don't think He's helping you out of it."

"Well, that's obvious," he huffed and lifted his hands.

"You know," Joe mused and nonchalantly stirred his coffee, "there's a way to acquire money I don't think you've tried."

"I've tried *everything*."

"Everything *humanly* possible," Joe contradicted and never looked up.

Joe's voice held a quiet strength that eased away some of the tension in Keith's gut. He leaned toward his friend.

"It'll not only provide you with enough to live on—probably more than enough—it'll also give you a more fulfilling life all the way around." Joe resumed his waffle eating as if he'd never been speaking.

"Well, are you going to tell me?" Keith prodded.

"Yep." Joe examined a forkful of egg and took the bite. "After I finish," he said with a mischievous smile.

Chapter Three

The Mercedes rolled to a stop a block from the strip of offices where Keith's firm was located. Jenny pulled down the sun visor and examined her appearance in the vanity mirror. A renewed surge of assurance swept aside all traces of anxiety. With her hair slicked straight back and no makeup, she didn't even resemble her usual meticulous image. The light dusting of dark powder underneath her eyes gave her a tired, browbeaten appearance. The faded jeans and smock top heightened the effect. Truth be known, Jenny felt exactly like she looked.

But she couldn't let that halt her. She was a woman on a mission and wouldn't stop until she had her answer.

Jenny turned off the ignition, removed the keys, and dropped them into her smock's pocket. She retrieved a second set of keys from her Louis Vuitton bag. They jingled as she dropped them into her smock pocket atop the thin, latex gloves. Jenny tucked her purse under the passenger seat and eyed the strip of offices, spotting the one she recognized well. At this distance, she couldn't read the writing on the door, but she knew what it said: "Simon, Lane, and Rothingham: Financial Advisors." Few would believe the millions of dollars the representatives invested every year. The understated office certainly didn't depict the wealth that had been created from the team of trusty investors. Keith Richardson was one of them, and Jenny and he both hoped his name would eventually be on the door.

Jenny knew that if Simon, Lane, or Rothingham found out Keith was philandering it would compromise his chances of any advancement. This investment firm was like Queen Victoria when it came to employee morals. They wanted no part of anything or anyone who would taint their reputation.

And I don't want any part of it either, Jenny thought. Her eyes stung as she thought of Celia Rothingham. Unfortunately, that tall brunette wasn't as uptight about morals as her father. However, "Daddy dear" seemed oblivious to his daughter's eye for Keith.

But even if Celia was the one, Jenny didn't want a divorce. Not at all. When she confronted Keith, Jenny prayed he would confess, beg for forgiveness, and want to move forward in their marriage. She'd be willing to do anything...go to counseling...admit the areas *she'd* failed.

God knows I've failed.

"Oh, God, help me," Jenny prayed and recalled nagging more than not the last few months.

She got out of the Mercedes and locked the door. The 8:00 city traffic hummed and honked in rhythm with her sneakers as they struck the pavement. She made it to the strip of offices in less than a minute and ducked beside the doughnut shop on the end. The smell of fresh pastries tugged at Jenny's appetite, but she admonished herself against even thinking about indulging. That chocolate almond ice cream was going to cost her big during her next workout. The last thing she needed was to add to it.

Jenny strode down the narrow alley, passing several metal doors before pausing in front of the one that was her target. She eyed the simple box to the right of the door frame and held her breath before punching in the code that would deactivate the alarm. Many times she'd stood with Keith as he pressed the numbers. Jenny hoped her memory didn't fail her this time.

Only a few employees knew the code, and those few were not supposed to share the number with anyone—not even a spouse. While Keith hadn't violated this policy, Jenny had been with him enough to recall the combination.

"I hope," she whispered and inserted her hand into her pocket. She fingered the extra set of keys Keith kept in the nightstand. Jenny wasn't supposed to have the key to the building. Then again, she wasn't supposed to be impersonating a cleaning lady either. But this was a desperate moment. Jenny had to find out who *she* was. Period. Once that task was complete, she'd find the woman's husband, if she were married, and do everything in her power to sabotage the adulterous relationship. From there, she'd scrape together the pieces of her marriage and try to rebuild what had been lost. That is, if Keith were willing.

Tears pooled in her eyes. Jenny dashed them aside.

Feeling like the criminal of the decade, she pulled the set of thin gloves from her pocket and wiggled her fingers into them. Jenny pressed her trembling finger against the buttons and panted with every beep. She'd clipped her sculptured nails short and removed the polish. Now the tips of her fingers felt oddly vulnerable against the keypad.

After the sixth number, a green message scrolled across the tiny screen: "Alarm deactivated."

Her shoulders sagging, she rested her forehead against the brick wall and closed her eyes until something touched her leg. Jenny stiffened as a million insane possibilities raced through her mind...including an attacker.

But he'd have to be really short, she thought. Her eyes popped open. A scrawny cat made another pass at her leg and meowed piteously.

Jenny shifted away from the brick wall and covered her chest with her hand. "You scared me to death," she accused, then covered her mouth and looked toward one end of the alley and then the other.

The cat howled and stared up at her with enough hunger to incite a hard-hearted ogre to find a can of tuna or at least a piece of bologna. As if that weren't bad enough, the critter was nearly an exact twin to a cat Jenny had as a child: solid black with a white-tipped nose and two paws that were touched in white. Her sister Elaine had run over Boots the day she got her first car. Jenny had cried herself to sleep that night.

"Oooh," she said. "I don't have time right now. Look. Stay here. When I come back out, I'll go buy you a can of cat food. Okay?"

"Meow!" the feline accused.

After a fierce sniff, Jenny concentrated on the door and refused to allow the cat to sway her. Time was wasting. She inserted a key into the door, turned the knob, and slipped into the financial firm's petite kitchen.

The place didn't open until nine. Since it was early, Jenny had banked on being the only one here. The dead silence confirmed her assumption. The place was hers. All hers. She would scour Keith's office. There had to be a clue that would implicate the other woman. He'd done a remarkable job hiding any evidence at home. Not even one suit pocket provided a trace of a clue. But Jenny figured Keith would never imagine she'd go this far. Logic insisted he couldn't have been as careful at the office.

After closing and locking the door, Jenny maneuvered through the kitchen and down the broad hallway. The smell of furniture oil and a faint trace of expensive potpourri added to the ambiance of money in the making.

She paused at Keith's door, eased it open, stepped inside. A well of emotions rushing through her, Jenny tightened her mouth and swallowed hard. Everywhere she looked she encountered the man she loved—from his bold choice of modern art claiming the walls to the rust-colored leather couch in the corner. His collection of antique hats hung on the coat tree…one had been worn by Fred Astaire himself.

But this is the man who's cheating on me! The brusque reminder dashed aside the poignant moment. Her face heated. She clenched her jaw. After a moment of blinding rage, Jenny regained her focus and surged forward.

Chapter Four

Joe poured some fresh coffee into Keith's cup and pushed it back toward him. Then he filled his own. With tiny, curling clouds swirling over his hot coffee, Joe walked to the window and gazed into the morning darkness.

Keith pushed his coffee aside. Dollops of dark liquid splashed from the rim to create tiny puddles atop the oak table. "Well, Dr. Joe," he prompted, "are you going to tell me about this miracle cure, or are you going to make me wait until dinner to find out?"

Swiveling from the window, Joe shot his friend a broad grin. "The thing I like the most about you is your patience."

"Well, I can only take so much!" Keith declared. "Watching you chew a waffle like a satisfied lion while you know I'm waiting with bated breath isn't exactly my idea of a good time."

Joe laughed out loud. "I didn't know lions ate waffles."

With a threatening growl, Keith stood and stepped around the table.

"Okay. Okay." Joe held up one hand. "I give. You're meaner than me!"

"Don't forget it! I'll act like Charlie and Rick and put salt in the Bunn." Keith pointed at Joe's nose and couldn't stop his lips from twitching.

"So *that's* what those two scoundrels were up to yesterday!" Joe exclaimed.

"Yeah, and I've got a hunch they have all sorts of other tricks up their sleeves," Keith threatened.

Joe sipped his coffee and peered over the steam. "I'm not scared of them. Their bark's worse than their bite. They can't even fish without getting tangled in their own hooks. Did you notice Rick's eyebrow?"

"Yeah. What happened?"

Joe set his coffee cup on the windowsill. His lips quivered. "Charlie 'caught' him," Joe drew invisible quotation marks in the air, "in the eyebrow!"

Keith resisted a roll of laughter. He looked down, bit his lips, and made a monumental job of mopping up the spilled coffee with his paper napkin.

Joe's snicker catapulted Keith into outright hilarity. "We shouldn't laugh," he protested. "I know that had to cause a truck-load of hurt."

"Or at least a *boatload*," Joe wheezed.

"Ah, man, that was bad," Keith complained and snickered harder.

"I know. I know. But I promise, you should have *seen* Rick. He came into the shop with a bandage the size of South Dakota, and he was madder than a hornet. I'm not sure he's over it yet!"

Keith rubbed his eyes. "I'd forgotten what a couple of characters those two are. Not a dull moment."

"Yep, but they love each other. They're like brothers."

"I know...I know." Keith stepped toward the trash can and dropped the damp napkin inside. It landed on an empty juice bottle and slipped from sight. *Just like my money*, Keith thought. He sobered and looked at Joe.

Joe's smile diminished. "I guess it's time to talk money," he said. He untied his butcher apron and draped it over a nearby chair. "Let's get down to business." Joe's kind, gray eyes couldn't have held more compassion. "I wasn't just trying to jerk you around when I waited until I finished eating. I wanted you to see something first."

Keith stepped toward his friend. A flicker of hope leaped to full flame. The guy seemed convinced that his plan would work, and Keith was willing to try anything short of bank robbery.

Joe motioned Keith to stand beside him at the window while he turned off the kitchen light. The distant glow from the living room lamp offered the only reprieve from inky darkness.

With the kitchen cloaked in shadows, the yard became more visible. At five forty, the eastern horizon was barely pale with a hint of an approaching sunrise.

"I don't know if you can see it now," Joe said, "but remember I pointed out the tilled field when we drove up yesterday?" Joe leaned toward the window. His intense stance suggested he saw the prepared soil despite the darkness.

"Yes," Keith replied.

Joe and Marcy lived in the western limit of Washington's wheat country. Their farm consisted of twenty acres of land surrounded by trees on one side and a new elementary school on the other. Their clean log cabin, with its manicured front yard, claimed half an acre. The rest of the land had been cleared for crops. Yesterday

Joe had explained that for the past two years he and Marcy had taken up her parents' mantle and raised fifteen acres of wheat.

Keith strained to see the fields but detected nothing but what the lone security light's hazy glow revealed…a few trees, a picnic table, and a doghouse with a snoozing German Shepherd halfway emerged.

"There's a tried-and-true way to get money," Joe said, and Keith strained to follow the implication that was eluding him. "And, really, it might seem odd at first to an investment guru like yourself. But I can guarantee it will provide you with enough to live on and more. On top of that, you won't have to slave for it."

"Okay." Keith leaned closer.

Joe reached for his coffee on the windowsill, then took a sip. "It can be summed up in one word," he continued.

"One word?" Keith's eyes widened. "You're joking, right? You've never explained anything in one word! Your ingredients for a double latte have more words than the Declaration of Independence."

"Ha, ha!" Joe mocked and gazed back out the window. "Seriously, it's just *one word*," he insisted.

"Robbery?" Keith prodded.

Joe shot him a glance that dripped with sarcasm, even in the shadows.

"Embezzlement?" Keith offered.

Joe narrowed his eyes. "Get real."

"I'm almost ready to try anything."

"C'mon, Keith! It doesn't have anything to do with breaking any laws. It has more to do with breaking the cycle of selfishness."

"Oh great!" Keith crossed his arms. "Here comes the Dr. Phil speech!"

"No speeches," Joe said. "Just a life lesson. One I learned when

I was in your shoes. And I can assure you that my shoes didn't fit any better than yours."

Keith wiggled his toes. The boots were still loose in all the same places. "Okay, so shoot. I've waited long enough."

"You're sure you're ready?" Joe snapped on the light and looked all the way into Keith's soul.

He squirmed. Joe was serious. Dead serious. And whatever this was he had a hunch it was going to involve more than a word.

Finally Keith pulled together the fortitude to nod. "Ready."

"The word is...'giving.'"

"Giving?" Keith blurted. "Are you nuts?" The question hopped through his mind and popped out of his mouth before Keith had the chance to censor it.

Joe threw back his head and laughed. While Keith was assured Joe wasn't offended, he was far from certain this one word was going to change his world.

"Maybe you didn't hear me," Keith sputtered. "I'm nearly broke! I lost all of Jenny's inheritance. I'm up to my eyeballs in debt. And your one-word suggestion for all our financial ills is to give what little money we have *away?*" Keith raised both hands and wondered why he'd even come to Seattle. Joe had apparently been listening to one-too-many over-the-edge shyster evangelists who conned their listeners with unrealistic promises.

"Listen, Keith." Joe gripped his arm. "I've discovered a principle that *works!*" His fingers tightened. "I'm really not crazy." His alert, intelligent gaze attested to his claim.

"Okay, let's hear the details, then," Keith heard himself say, and he decided he must be more desperate than even *he* realized.

"I call it the Cycle of Giving." Joe released Keith's arm. "Believe me, when Rick told me about it, I was as skeptical as you. But I was as desperate as you too."

Keith wrinkled his forehead.

"Okay, maybe not *quite* as desperate as you...but definitely in need of some cash flow. Some quiet voice in me suggested that I'd tried everything else, so what was the harm of trying this as well. So I decided to go for it. It all boils down to giving to get *to give again*. That's the whole cycle."

"Sounds like one of those infomercial videos you can order at midnight—but the thing costs $200—and the only people getting rich are the ones collecting your payment." Keith gripped his forehead. "I just don't see this working. There's no way to trace it...no hard figures." He lowered his hand and repeated, "I just don't see it!"

"I'm a coffee shop owner—not a financial whiz." Joe shrugged. "I don't know how it works. All I know is it's worked big in my life. If this principle wasn't within my mental and spiritual reach, I wouldn't be practicing it. I'd be sitting next to you talking to the bankruptcy attorneys."

Keith winced and stroked his brow. "Ouch! That one hurt. I think you hooked me in the eyebrow. Why not just go for my pupil?"

Joe sputtered. "Sorry," he said, and squeezed Keith's shoulder. "All I'm sayin' is that as crazy as it may seem, it's worked for me and *worked big.*" He nodded. "You see, giving is actually a way of getting back. But the real key is that you don't stop there. You're not out for greed or self-promotion. You want to keep the cycle going by continuing to give to help others and promote God's work. Personal wealth is not your goal."

Sighing, Keith turned toward the table and picked up his coffee cup. He took a long swallow and eyed his breakfast plate. It was as empty as his checking account.

Joe had been a good friend for many years. He'd never done anything daft—at least not anything that mattered—unless you counted the time he accidentally put diesel in his gas-guzzling truck and gagged the engine. Other than that, Joe had proven himself dependable, stable, and forever full of sound decisions…right down to the woman he'd married. Marcy was a jewel.

Keith sighed and faced his friend. "At this point a solid piece of advice is exactly what I need. Either that or an exorcist," he added under his breath.

Joe's laughter bounced off the walls. He plopped his coffee on the table, grabbed a chair, turned it around, straddled it, and dropped into the seat. Still chuckling, he rested his arms along the back and looked up at Keith. "Well, I can't help you with an exorcist, but I can promise that if you'll listen and do what I say, you'll be seeing black rather than red. You'll have enough money and a better climate at home."

Keith blinked and decided he really didn't have a choice. Everything else *he'd* tried had failed. "Okay. You win," he said. "I'll hear you out."

"Good. But really, I think it's best to let the soil do the talking."

"The soil?"

"Yep. You're in those work clothes for a reason," Joe claimed.

Keith looked down at the borrowed sweatshirt and jeans. "I am?"

Joe nodded. "We've got some farming to do."

Chapter Five

Jenny checked her diamond-studded Rolex. The time didn't shock her as much as the fact that she was wearing her expensive watch. Housekeepers didn't usually own such luxuries. She unlatched the clasp, dropped the timepiece into her smock pocket, and lambasted herself for the oversight. But then she still didn't know what time it was. Jenny jerked the watch from the pocket and absorbed the time. A slow wash of horror warmed her. She'd somehow let time slip away. The financial firm opened in just ten minutes. Employees would be arriving any second. Or maybe they'd already begun arriving!

She gripped the edge of Celia Rothingham's desk and listened. The faint sound of the back door opening preceded the tap of high heels on tile. Jenny picked up the mound of papers she'd pulled from Celia's desk and shoved them back into the drawer. When Keith's office provided no clues whatsoever, Jenny refused to accept defeat. She was irrevocably convinced her man was having an affair. All his behavior pointed to exactly that. He was just better than the average guy at hiding his tracks.

Once she had exited his office, Jenny decided to move to the next room on her list: Celia Rothingham's. No one would ever miss that the financial wizard was female...all the way female... right down to her long legs, high heels, and short skirts. From what Jenny understood, she worked magic with other people's money. She also turned heads everywhere she went. A few times Jenny had caught Keith turning *her* head. But Keith seemed oblivious to the woman and claimed he never noticed her.

Yeah right! Jenny fumed before silently sliding the desk drawer into place. But a second before the drawer closed, she caught sight of a photo lodged between the drawer and the desk. With the sound of high heels clicking around the kitchen, Jenny simultaneously yanked on the picture and looked toward the hallway. The photo ripped loose on the third pull. Jenny's eager gaze devoured the images of two people: her husband and Celia at the company Christmas party.

Celia was wearing a Santa hat, holding a glass of champagne, and sitting in Keith's lap. As usual, her short skirt revealed more of her thighs than it covered. Keith was looking squarely at the camera, his eyes round, his mouth gaping. Jenny remembered that expression well. It was the same shocked expression she'd captured on camera the year she caught him wrapping her birthday present...the diamond watch now riding in her smock pocket.

A hard tremor started at Jenny's knees and swept upward. Her eyes blurred. Even though she'd searched hard for any clues and was determined to find some, she'd rather have found none and been surprised to learn that her husband was innocent. But this photo was a long way from innocent. And Celia was a long way from looking unhappy.

She even looks better with Keith than I do, Jenny pined. Celia's tall, dark beauty complemented Keith to perfection. And for the first time in her life, Jenny felt like a pale, mousy has-been—not easy to swallow for a former Miss Oregon.

Jenny didn't hear the staccato footsteps until they were feet away. Her eyes wide, she gazed toward the ajar door. Fortunately, the echo of more footsteps approached from the other direction. "Good morning, Miss Rothingham," a cheerful female voice chirped. "I've made coffee."

"Oh great, Lori," Ceila's husky voice mingled with a yawn. "I was up late last night. I need all the boost I can get. Do you mind fixing me a cup? I'll be in my office."

"Of course not," Lori agreed. "Oh listen, the alarm system was off when I got here."

"Was the door locked?" Celia asked.

"Yes."

"I guess somebody forgot to turn it on again last night. I'll tell Dad."

Jenny shoved the photo into her pocket. Her gaze darted around the room. Hot beads of sweat erupted along her forehead as she searched for a closet or corner in which to hide. The only logical place she spotted was behind the drapes. As Celia's footsteps paused outside the doorway, Jenny scurried the few feet to the curtains. How she managed to scramble onto the waist-high ledge was anybody's guess. Once she stopped the scramble, she was wedged in the farthest corner, her knees to her chest, her arms locked around her legs. Being petite and mousy did have its advantages.

As the door sighed inward, the footsteps grew closer. Jenny squeezed her eyes shut, hugged her legs tightly, and rested her forehead against her knees. She held her breath and prayed like a maniac.

Celia's footsteps stopped.

Jenny slowly released her breath and silently panted.

"Oh my word!" Celia exclaimed. "I found it. I can't believe it! I've been looking all over for..."

Her eyes snapping open, Jenny lifted her head. Curiosity demanded she inch aside the curtain just enough to see Celia. The red-lipped brunette, her brow wrinkled, held a torn photo.

With the smell of Celia's jasmine perfume commanding the room, Jenny slowly straightened her legs and fumbled inside both her smock pockets. The photo was not to be found. *I must have missed my pocket!* Jenny blinked back tears of panic.

"But how did it get..." Celia mused.

Jenny stared at the curtain and wished for X-ray vision. But that only happened in movies. If she was going to see Celia, she'd have to peel aside the curtain once more. But even the thought of touching the curtain terrified Jenny.

"That's odd," Celia whispered, and Jenny was forced to face her fear.

The curtain trembled between her fingers as she nudged aside the folds.

Celia was examining her desk. When she focused on the cracked drawer, Jenny's heart hammered at the base of her throat. A roll of nausea nearly overtook her, and she feared she'd faint and fall to the floor for a big, revealing moment that might cost Keith his job.

The brunette pulled out the drawer and eyed the disheveled papers. "Oh my word," she breathed, "somebody's been..." She dropped the photo into the desk's center and hurried toward the door.

"Lori!" she squawked. "I think we've had a prowler!"

Rick McDugal always said Lake Sammamish was the mistress of the morning. This morning was no exception. In the predawn shadows, the smell of water and fish wafting through the mist promised a catch he and Charlie would brag about for years. There was a whale of a bass waiting for his chrome-tipped lure. He just knew it.

Rick glanced at his compadre, who was methodically preparing that blasted bamboo pole he always insisted upon bringing. Charlie hauled it with them on every fishing trip since he'd met his wife, Li. He vowed the nuisance was his good luck charm. Admittedly, he did catch a few fish on it nearly every time they went out, but what he caught on the pole never matched the monsters Rich hauled in on his rod and reel.

Meanwhile, Charlie'd tangled the pole's hook in more brush than should be legal and ripped a hole in Rick's fishing hat. Two months ago, he even embedded the hook in Rick's eyebrow. Now his eyebrow sported a chewed up, half-gone look, and Rick figured he'd go to his grave with that scar.

When Charlie had the squirming worm hooked just the way he wanted, he released the line. It swung like a crazed pendulum between the friends, and Rick leaned away from it while touching his good eyebrow. He bumped the lantern, which cast eerie shadows upon Charlie's profile and brought back memories of the pain. Rick wasn't in the mood to have his good eyebrow ripped off this morning.

"There she is!" Charlie chirped. "One of the finest worms in the state, and she's got a whopper of a perch on her list."

Just put the thing in the water, Rick thought.

With a smudge of weak, gray light on the eastern horizon, Charlie flicked the pole and the hook dropped into the water. The weight's gentle splash announced the deed complete.

Rick's eyebrows relaxed. He rubbed his hands along the front of his fishing vest and picked up his rod and reel from beside his chair. The small barge had been his and Charlie's joint investment. So far they'd enjoyed it immensely, if you didn't count the day they rammed it into the loading dock.

"You know, bamboo's one of the strongest poles out there," Charlie said.

With a grunt, Rick acknowledged Charlie's claim. The guy said something like that every trip. Didn't he think Rick would remember it after time number 2,341? Rick spotted the exact place he wanted to cast his lure and didn't give Charlie's bamboo another thought.

"I'm not worried about catching a big one on her," Charlie continued. "That little pole can hold up to a twenty pounder."

"Yeah…as long as you hook him in the eyebrow," Rick mumbled under his breath.

"I knew you were in a bad mood this morning," Charlie accused.

Rick glanced toward his friend's deeply lined face. His blue eyes looked downright beady in the lantern's light. Rick would have felt guilty for the jab except it was hard to feel guilty when you were missing part of an eyebrow.

"And there you are bringing up the accident again. When are you ever going to let it rest?" Charlie gazed toward Rick's mangled brow.

"I'm not grouchy," Rick snapped and rubbed his gritty eyes. He'd forgotten how many times a baby could wake up in the night until his daughter came home a couple of days ago with her two-month-old.

"And when your eyebrow gets ripped to smithereens, then *you* can talk." Rick clicked his reel with a vengeance and threw the line close to the bank. He'd caught a ten-pound bass in that exact spot last fall. A repeat performance would sure go a long way to waking him up and chasing the cobwebs from his mind.

"Your eyes look baggy," Charlie commented. "Did you lose another night's sleep?"

"Yeah. Bev didn't go home last night either."

"Did you say it was money problems?"

"I guess. Money's tight. They're fighting. That means I get serenaded by my granddaughter all night. How long has it been since you had colic?"

Charlie grunted.

"That's got to be the worst state of existence in the world...at least little Leandra lets on like it is."

"I guess Keith Richardson's got the same trouble."

Rick cut Charlie a hard glance. "What, colic?"

"No, man, money problems."

"Oh. Yeah. Right. You can say that again. He didn't look very good yesterday, did he?"

"Bad. Real bad," Charlie agreed. "Never seen him so low."

"Wonder what's going to become of him?"

"Don't know. Hate to see the kid like that. I was wondering about asking Li to talk to him."

"Your wife? What for?"

"The bamboo, man!" His eyes wide, Charlie pointed to his pole.

Rick tightened his jaw and didn't even try to understand. He wasn't in the mood for understanding anything anyway. Instead, he adjusted his fishing hat, wiped the cool mist from his face, and concentrated on working his lure. Bamboo was Charlie's answer to everything. He wouldn't be surprised if the man thought it could cure colic. Rick yawned and hoped his daughter and her husband got their act together soon. He couldn't take much more.

Chapter Six

Keith followed Joe from the kitchen and into the utility room that smelled of clean clothes. Joe paused beside the back door, decked in eyelet curtains, and peered into the dawn-laced shadows. He flipped on the back-porch light and said, "It's misting."

"What a shocker," Keith mocked. "Imagine, rain in Washington."

Joe chuckled and turned toward a row of hooks near the door. He pulled off a couple of oil-smeared baseball caps and handed one to Keith. "Nothing fancy," he said, "but it'll keep the rain outta your eyes."

"Thanks." Keith slipped on the hat and followed Joe's lead by reaching for one of the thin rain ponchos hanging near the hats.

"Now we're good to go."

Keith offered a thumbs up. The two men traipsed onto the back deck, their boots thumping against the damp wood.

A cautious "Woof!" preceded the appearance of the German shepherd, his ears pricked, his tail stiff.

"Hey, Spot!" Joe encouraged. "It's only me, ol' boy."

The dog lowered his ears, wagged his tail, and hurried toward Joe while sizing up Keith.

"This is my friend, Keith," Joe explained. "You remember him from yesterday, don't you?"

Keith extended his hand while Spot determined whether he was a good guy or his next meal. With a cautious wave of his tail, Spot took Keith off the menu and allowed him the privilege of an ear-scratch. "What a name," Keith said and straightened.

"Yep." Joe laughed. "That was Marcy's idea. She's got a wacky streak or two."

"Well, she married you, didn't she?" Keith said and punched Joe in the arm.

"Wow, thanks," Joe drawled. "I love you too."

"Ah, you do, man?" Keith draped his arm across Joe's shoulder. "I never knew!"

"Get away from me!" Joe shoved at his friend, and Keith's laughter mingled with the whisper of a breeze stirring the surrounding trees. The drizzle swooshed against Keith's cheeks with a rash of cold pricks, and the wind carried the smells of spring and damp earth. The sun had inched closer to exposure, but the clouds only allowed a feeble blush. Nevertheless, the promise of a new day encouraged Keith. There was life on the horizon.

As he followed Joe toward the field, Keith gazed at the acres of plowed earth. Joe said he was going to let the soil do the talking, whatever that meant. Keith sensed that it had something to do with that Cycle of Giving business. A new plague of doubts attacked him. He'd heard of good people getting sucked into cults and all sorts of twisted stuff. He hoped for Joe's sake—and his own—that this was not one of those deals. Keith needed some answers that would work. And Joe didn't need to be tangled up in any nonsense. If he was, Keith decided he would drag him out, even if Joe was kicking and screaming.

The boots slipped on Keith's heels a bit as they trudged across damp grass and closer to the field. Another whisk of a breeze sneaked under his poncho. It billowed up, and droplets of cold moisture dotted his hands and assaulted the back of his neck. A shiver rattled his teeth.

Joe shot him a sideways look and grinned. "Welcome home."

Keith smiled. "Really."

The men stopped on the edge of the field. With every passing minute the countryside grew more visible. Now Keith detected a low-lying fog that oozed from the Cascade Mountains. The white mist hugged the earth like a fluffy, white blanket and melted into the earth, stretching on for ages.

"Marcy was raised on this farm," Joe explained as he crossed his arms beneath the poncho. "I took her to the city when we married and promised her one day we'd have our own farm. Then her parents wanted to do some traveling and offered us the place. I think Marcy would have killed me if I'd said no. Now she's a happy camper, and I get to commute to the coffee shop. But I found out I'm not just an ordinary coffee shop owner." He lifted his head a fraction. "I've got farmer in me."

An ancient longing overtook Keith. He didn't question the urge or try to stop it. Without a second's pause, Keith stooped and dug his fingers into the freshly tilled soil. The top layer was damp. Beneath, the earth was pregnant with life.

I wonder what this has to do with giving, he mused again. Keith gazed across the field. The farm was complete with a tractor and a big, red barn.

The mist grew to a patter, and drops of rain dripped from the bill of his hat. Keith knew from experience that the mist would most likely turn into a full-fledged rain by afternoon. He glanced toward the east. The sun had undoubtedly crested the horizon, but only a gray glow attested to the event.

"Twenty acres…lots of dirt," Keith commented. He allowed the earth to slip through his fingers, then lifted them to his nose and inhaled. The scent took him back to creation, to the most basic of human survival.

"We farmers don't call it dirt," Joe corrected with a smile in his voice. "It's *soil*…rich in organisms. Having the right organic mix will decide whether the crop is strong or weak." He knelt beside Keith.

"Excuse me. *Soil*," Keith said and cut a glance toward Joe. "I'm a city boy, remember? The only thing I know about farming is that the chicken comes before the egg. Or is it the other way around?"

"I have no idea. I don't do chickens," Joe said.

"Humph." Keith traced a tiny trough through the earth. "You're really into this, aren't you? I thought you just went to some farm store, bought a bag of seed, threw it on the ground, and prayed for rain—which isn't that much of a stretch when you live in Washington."

The gentle breeze pushed harder, and a puff of wet wind blasted Keith's face.

"You can say *that* again," Joe said, rubbing at his eyes. "There's actually a science to this. What we do before we plant affects the crop." New enthusiasm fused with his words. "When we first took over the farm, we decided to raise wheat like Marcy's parents had. But we did a test patch to better learn the ropes. We planted just enough to yield a couple hundred bushels."

"Oh, *that's* all," Keith mocked. "Like, what would anybody do with 200 bushels of wheat anyway?"

"It's really not all that many for a wheat farmer." Joe gazed toward the road as a Chevrolet slowed and turned into the driveway.

"That Marcy?" Keith asked.

"Yes. I'm going to have to go back in soon and do the egg thing. You devoured enough for you and her."

Keith nodded. "Yeah. Sorry 'bout that…just not sorry enough not to do it."

"Right. I could tell," Joe said through a chipped-tooth smile before his attention shifted back to the earth. He stood, walked toward a nearby oak, picked up a shovel propped there. "Although we make a good living," he said on the way back, "we're making a fortune in experience!"

Joe walked to where the grass was creeping toward the soil and motioned Keith to follow. Keith stood and neared his friend, who sank the shovel into the ground and turned over a scoop. Beneath the thin layer of new moisture the soil was dry. Joe bent down and picked up a handful.

"You've heard the phrase 'fertile soil'? That means the soil can give birth. It's alive with what plants need to grow." He opened his hand, and the clump stood strong and proud against his palm. "This is the stuff that strong plants are made of. They can grow like crazy…resist pests and diseases. The stronger they are, the bigger the crop."

Keith listened and tried to squeeze some money into—or out of—this whole thing. So far, he was not computing. Joe himself said they weren't getting rich. Keith crossed his arms under the poncho and squinted his eyes.

Peering at his friend, Joe continued, "I guess it's a lot like a cake recipe," he mused, "except instead of stirring in eggs and flour and sugar, we're stirring in nitrogen, phosphorus, and potassium."

"And exactly what product has all that?" Keith cautiously queried.

Joe laughed.

"Please don't tell me the M-word is in my future." Keith placed his hands on his hips and imagined all sorts of gross scenarios— and odors. He also relived the graphic memory of the day he fell headlong into a pile of it at his grandfather's Alabama farm. He'd been nine and almost never got the stench out of his hair.

"I thought you didn't know anything about farming!" Joe crumbled the clump and allowed it to sift through his fingers, only to dig into the earth and pick up more. "Over a million seeds per acre," he said, his attention on the earth. "But you might as well throw the seed to the wind unless you take care of the soil."

The mist gradually turned to a steady drizzle, as if someone were slowly turning the faucet in a shower stall. Joe held his hands out and let the water wash away the soil.

Keith mopped at a stream that slipped down the side of his face.

"Plus," Joe continued, "you have to do the hard labor. If you leave the ground unturned and compacted, the seed doesn't stand a chance. The soil has to be broken up."

"Cultivated," Keith stated.

"Ah…the city boy knows more than he's admitting." Joe stood and rubbed his hands against his jeans. Streaks of dirt smudged faded blue.

"I've watched the Discovery Channel a time or two," Keith wryly claimed.

"Good for you." Joe walked his shovel back to the oak and propped it where he found it.

Keith didn't bother to mention his grandfather's corn farm or the numerous summers he spent there as a kid. But aside from the manure business, he remembered more about playing in the hay barn than anything else.

After hurrying back to Keith, Joe whacked his back. "Let's go in. Marcy's going to be howling for eggs."

"But—" Keith began.

Joe lifted his hand. "We're just pausing before verse two. Let's shake off the rain and get Marcy fed first, okay?"

With the clap of Celia's footsteps echoing down the hallway, Jenny stiffened with indecision. She pulled her knees closer and squeezed her eyes tight. Her first instinct suggested she should hop from the broad windowsill and race willy-nilly to freedom. A more logical voice suggested this was the reason she'd disguised herself. Jenny had fully planned to get into the firm and out before anyone came. But just in case she got caught, she'd donned the cleaning lady look.

Okay, be calm, she told herself and prayed for a dose of courage.

With the sound of Celia's elevated voice mingling with Lori's questions, Jenny pulled aside the curtain, scouted the empty office, and dropped from the ledge. Her unsteady legs nearly buckled, but Jenny forced herself to scurry to the door. She peered toward the voices coming from the kitchen.

"And my drawer is a mess! I *know* there's been someone in here.

And you said the alarm wasn't set, either. Maybe it wasn't that somebody forgot—but that a prowler hacked into it."

"This is creepy," Lori said. "Maybe we should call the police."

Police! Jenny gripped the door jamb to stop herself from falling to her knees. Panting, she looked up one end of the hall, then the other. Her gaze fell upon a door marked "Ladies." She bolted toward the door, glancing over her shoulder with every other step. Just as she slipped into the room, she caught a glimpse of Celia's fiery red suit.

A trickle of sweat slipped down Jenny's spine as she desperately scoured the room for an escape. But there were no windows, and she was too big to squeeze down the sink drain. Lori and Celia's voices neared the ladies' room, and Jenny wondered if they'd seen her slip inside. She tiptoed to a stall, closed and latched the door, crawled onto the toilet, and held her breath. When the voices receded, she closed her eyes and released her breath.

Okay, now what? she thought. Jenny certainly couldn't crouch in the stall all day. *Get out of here!* the primal urge to escape sent her into a whirl that made the stall spin.

"No, stop!" she whispered and pressed her fists against her temples. *Cleaning lady. Cleaning lady*, she reminded herself and forced her mind to focus.

The memory of the twin doors on the front of the sink cabinet sent her into action. There were often cleaning supplies behind sink doors. All Jenny needed was a can of Lysol and a cloth to complete her disguise and give her a one-way ticket to freedom. Jenny stepped down. Her fingers shook so violently she could hardly slide open the door lock. After two fumbled attempts, the task was complete.

She stumbled to the sink, opened the cabinet and examined the contents. Two rolls of tissue, a stack of paper hand towels, a small commode plunger, and a container of Liquid Plumber. Not one can of Lysol.

Jenny blinked and swallowed hard. Being a prowler wasn't all it was cracked up to be. Desperately she snatched up a stack of paper hand towels and rested her chin on the top to balance them.

Just make it to the kitchen, she admonished. *Once there, you're home free.*

She edged open the door with her empty hand. While tense female voices ebbed and flowed from Celia's office, Jenny forced her feet to obey her demands and not dash to the back door. But a leisurely stroll didn't exactly fit the moment either. She compromised with a brisk gait and only looked over her shoulder once before entering the kitchen.

But that one glance cost her. When she shifted her attention back toward the kitchen, it was too late to stop a direct hit with a tall, thin man whom Jenny recognized all too well. Rothingham Sr.! And to make matters worse, he was carrying tea. A jumble of scalding liquid, paper towels, and flailing arms accompanied a round of masculine grunts.

"Can't you watch where you're going!" he finally boomed.

As the final paper towels tumbled from Jenny's grip, she gaped up at her husband's boss—all six feet of him. For a second she feared he'd recognize her, but she saw nothing in his features but turmoil and hot anger.

"You idiot!" Rothingham shook droplets from both hands while looking down at his stained white shirt. Beads of amber liquid dotted his tie and the front of his suit. As usual, the man was dressed to the teeth—just like his daughter. Jenny never had come close to liking him. And in some twisted sort of way, the tea baptism stirred her humor.

A hysterical giggle erupted from Jenny before she could check it. Rothingham's face darkened to the no-control zone. Jenny gulped and finally gave in to the urge to run. She whipped around him, dashed across the kitchen, and hit the exit bar on the door.

The metal door banged open to the accompaniment of Rothingham's, "Come back here!"

"What's going on?" Celia's shriek fueled Jenny's speed.

Jenny's arms pumped in sequence with her legs as she raced down the alley. She didn't have to wonder if Rothingham would be chasing her. That man would track down a hungry orphan for a nickel.

Chapter Seven

Keith gazed out his bedroom window with his cell phone to his ear. He counted the fifth ring on Jenny's phone and wasn't surprised when the voice mail message kicked in. Frowning, Keith snapped his cell phone shut and pressed the antenna against his palm. It snapped back into its cylinder. Thoughtfully he pinched the end of the antenna and wondered why Jenny hadn't called him. He'd called her on a whim…maybe because he missed her. Keith wasn't really sure. He just knew he wanted to hear her voice. It was odd that she hadn't called since yesterday. Really odd. Not like Jenny at all.

He admired the Cascade Mountains in the distance. Snow sprinkled the slopes like powdered sugar on mounds of gray glaciers. The peaks looked as cold as Keith's gut felt. He wished his life was half as serene. But it wasn't. Not by a long shot.

He pressed his fingers against his eyes and knew Joe was so right. He *had* to tell Jenny. But how? Even his unsuccessful attempt to call hadn't been fueled by his desire to confess. Keith was still a long way from coming clean. The shame just wouldn't quit. And he couldn't bear the thought of Jenny knowing he'd so royally failed.

Keith dropped to the bed's quilted coverlet and flopped back onto the pillows. He stared at the ceiling and wished he and Jenny could have even half what Marcy and Joe had. The reason Keith was in his room was because he'd stumbled upon them in the kitchen in a lip-lock. Keith had gone to the restroom and returned to two married people really enjoying each other's company.

He'd silently excused himself and decided to call Jenny. Keith couldn't remember the last time he'd kissed her like that…and held her tight. An old longing seized him. Loneliness followed. He groaned and closed his eyes as the memories overtook him. "Jenny… Jenny…oh, Jenny," he breathed. "How can you ever forgive me?"

"I said come back here!" Rothingham's irate demand accompanied the pounding of his shoes against the alley.

With a whimper, Jenny glanced over her shoulder and stifled a scream. No matter how fast she was running, Keith's boss was gaining…and swiftly. Sweat trickled to the corner of her eye for a sting that matched the burning in her thighs. Jenny was in good shape, but this desperate sprint ranked above what she usually did.

As Rothingham neared, the alley seemed to grow longer, like a warped corridor in an endless nightmare. Gulping for air, Jenny frantically searched for some means of stopping him when a group of trash cans just ahead proved the perfect answer. Grinding her teeth, Jenny zoomed to the first trash can and heaved it to the ground. By the time the smelly contents spread across the alley, the second trash can was following. When she attacked the third one,

Jenny found it empty. She hurled it behind her and didn't bother to observe the results. The rumble and grunt of Rothingham hitting the ground followed by enraged curses were answer enough.

Jenny spanned the end of the alley and burst into the parking lot. She spotted her Mercedes still parked one block away. Nevertheless, she halted and spotted a stack of large, cardboard boxes sitting near a door marked "Employees Only." Jenny recalled the electronics and appliance store that was several doors down from the firm. A couple of the boxes looked like they belonged to mid-sized TVs…a perfect fit for a small woman. With another glance toward the alley, Jenny made a decision she hoped was the right one. Instead of racing for her car and having Rothingham potentially see it and her license plate, Jenny ducked toward the boxes. With a last, desperate glimpse toward the alley, she dropped to her knees, hunkered down, and pulled one of the boxes on top of her.

"Please, God," she huffed, "don't let him find me. Keith will *kill* me!" Jenny doubled her fists, stared at the tiny shafts of light that shot from beneath the box's edges, and tried to control her erratic breathing.

The crunch of irregular footsteps merged from the alley. Jenny bit the end of her tongue and swallowed another whimper. The smell of cardboard reminded her of the days she and Keith were moving to Detroit. They'd both had such high hopes that all their dreams were becoming a reality. She never imagined she'd find herself running from Keith's boss and hiding under a box near an alley.

As Rothingham neared, Jenny covered her face with her hands and counted his every breath while she held hers.

"Daddy! Daddy! Are you okay?" Celia's yelps accompanied the slap of high heels on pavement.

"Yeah. Fine," he growled.

"Oh no! You're bleeding!" Celia wailed. "Look! Blood is all over your shirt."

"It's just my lip," he complained.

"This is just awful! We're going to have to get you to a clinic. I think you need stitches."

Stitches! Jenny's eyes popped open. This was getting worse by the second.

"Forget me and my bloody lip. Do you see her anywhere? Help me look!"

Celia's footsteps tapped within feet of Jenny's box, which was growing more stifling by the second. A dull thud on top of the box sent Jenny into a spastic jump. Somehow she swallowed her squeal. Her heart hammering, she assumed the thud must be Celia on the prowl, and she was on the brink of being discovered.

"Hey! Something moved over here in these boxes!" Celia crowed.

The heavy approach of footsteps sealed Jenny's doom. Hot tears trickled to the corners of her mouth to christen the moment in a salty kiss.

A piteous "meow," accompanied by the pat of paws above Jenny's head explained the thud. *It must be Boots*, she thought.

"It's just a stupid cat," Rothingham growled.

"Well, I thought—"

"Can't you see those boxes are too small for a grown woman to fit into?"

Think again, Jenny thought and dashed at the tears while her shoulders sank toward her knees. She laid her hands on the concrete and heaved with the silent sobs that erupted from a well of relief.

A stream of ranting merged with Rothingham's retreating gait.

"Daddy—oh, Daddy—just *look* at you!" Celia exclaimed. "You're bleeding like crazy now. We've got to get you to a clinic."

"No! We've got to call the police first."

Jenny's head popped up.

Boots howled. He sounded as forlorn and scared as Jenny felt. He'd also served as the perfect distraction against her predators.

If I get out of here, she vowed, *I'll take you home with me and feed you…and—and buy you a cat bed and treat you like royalty!* With the decision made, Jenny waited until Celia's voice was but a faint irritation. Then she lifted the box.

Keith followed Joe through the entrance into Mac's Place. A tiny bell hung from the door and jangled when they entered. Keith relished the smell of freshly brewed gourmet coffee and familiar pastry loaded with coconut.

He'd barely hung up from trying to reach Jenny over an hour ago when Joe came into the bedroom and announced he was needed at work. It seemed there was a problem with the computer.

A young lady with skin as rich and dark as the finest Colombian brew helplessly looked up from the computerized cash register. "I'm so sorry, Joe," she said, shaking her head. "I know this is your day off." She gazed past Joe and flashed an apologetic glance at Keith.

Keith settled onto his favorite bar stool and grinned at Lila. She was a cute chick with almond-shaped eyes who resembled an exotic Ethiopian princess. Her faded blue jeans and butcher apron that read "Mac's Place" defied the princess possibilities.

"Not a problem," Joe replied.

"I've tried everything but kicking it." She backed away, stabbed a pen in her braided bun, and eyed the computer like it was The Beast from the book of Revelation.

"A good kick might be what it needs," Joe said through a chortle. "I know Marcy says I need one every now and again."

Lila's face relaxed into a smile.

"Go take care of the customers," Joe said, jerking his head toward the small line of sleepy-eyed regulars who were longingly gazing at the pot full of coffee. "If I can't get this baby to work, I'll pry the money drawer open, and we'll resort to the old-fashioned way of doing things." He wrinkled his nose and whispered, "We'll write out receipts."

The manager placed her hand over her chest and gasped, "No!"

"Oh yeah," Joe assured.

While Joe did the tango with the computer, Keith's attention trailed to the pastry case. Sure enough, there were croissant-looking confections that oozed cream from the middle and were topped with enough coconut to drive a man crazy. Keith remembered eating one of those with Jenny on their first date—if you could call it a date. He'd asked her to meet him here. By the time the coconut was gone, Keith knew he had to have another meeting with Jenny. The next time he picked her up and treated her to the best restaurant in Seattle.

Despite his big breakfast, Keith's taste buds ached as strongly as his heart. That's when he started lusting after the cappuccino Lila was whipping up. He'd only had one full mug of coffee this morning. And the shop's ambiance spurred him to relive the good times he'd shared over a mug.

"Just help yourself to whatever," Joe encouraged, and Keith glanced in his direction as he waved toward the pastry case.

"Was I that transparent?"

"Ah, I don't know. It was kinda hard to tell what you were thinking with all that drool dripping from your mouth."

Keith laughed and realized Joe now held a flat-ended screwdriver. He glared at the computerized machine like he meant business.

"You're really going to pry the drawer open?" Keith asked.

"Yep. It's time this thing learns who's boss."

Keith snickered and slid from his stool. "I'll be by the fire with my croissant." He lifted the wooden panel that allowed him access behind the counter. Soon Keith had a steaming cappuccino in one hand and a croissant-laden saucer in the other. He meandered between the tables and found an empty chair near the fireplace. He placed his treasures on the table and checked his watch.

Nearly eight, he mused. *That's eleven Jenny time. She should be up.* Keith pulled his cell phone from his belt. *She should have seen that I called even though I didn't leave a message.* He checked to see if he'd somehow missed a signal when she called. But there was no indication of a missed call or a new voice mail. A nagging worry troubled his soul, and Keith hoped his wife was okay.

"Thanks, Boss. You're the greatest," Lila's impassioned appreciation snared Keith's attention.

Joe, now nearing Keith's table, shot her one of his champion smiles. When she blew a kiss to Joe, Keith's brow wrinkled.

"Save it for your Uncle Rick," Joe said through a good-natured chuckle.

Keith glanced back at Lila, who was busily filling a mug as if nothing had happened. Joe grabbed the chair across from Keith, turned it backward, and straddled it, before plopping on it.

"She's a good kid," Joe said and set an icy cola on the table.

"She's a *good-lookin'* kid," Keith said. "Better not let Marcy see her throwing you kisses."

"Ah." Joe waved away the concern. "Marcy doesn't care. She knows it's all in jest. Besides, Lila is Rick's niece. I've known her for ages. She's like a little sister."

"Jenny would blow a fuse if somebody who looks like her blew me a kiss," Keith admitted. "And I don't care if she was fifteen years younger, and I knew her when she was born."

"Maybe Jenny just feels a little insecure in your relationship."

"A little!" Keith snorted and rolled his eyes. "Ya think?"

"There's a remedy for that, you know," Joe said, and stirred the soda with his straw.

"Do tell," Keith prodded.

Joe lifted his gaze and narrowed his eyes. "Put as much time into your marriage as you would your favorite hobby."

Keith twisted the gold band on his ring finger and recalled that clutch scene in Joe's kitchen and the fact that he'd cooked Marcy's breakfast. The man must be practicing what he preached. Problem was, Keith's only hobby lately was work, work, work, and more work.

"When a woman knows you worship the ground she walks on, she's less likely to worry about any rivals," Joe said.

A disgruntled humph escaped Keith, and he stuffed a gigantic bite of the croissant in his mouth. His taste buds applauded the move.

His heart remembered the scene. Jenny had dripped a dollop of coconut cream on her chin during that first meeting, and he'd wiped it away with his napkin. He'd wanted to kiss her then but refrained until their second date.

How something so electric could have spiraled into something so tragic left Keith reeling with pain. "Rival or no, she's probably going to drop me in the closest ditch when she finds out I lost her inheritance," he growled.

"Which brings us to another point," Joe said. "You've got to tell her." His keen gaze penetrated Keith's comfort zone.

"Yeah, I've heard that rumor," Keith mumbled.

"Soon." Joe pushed aside his Coke. His voice was heated with urgency.

Keith rubbed his thigh, curled his fingertips around his knee cap, and squeezed. "So you and Marcy really plant wheat and grow it? How do you make time for all that work?"

Joe blinked.

The subject change was as abrupt and awkward as Keith's tone was stiff.

Chapter Eight

"I'm sorry, Ma'am," the cashier said, "but your card has been declined."

"Excuse me?" Jenny said while eyeing the cat carrier that rocked in the shopping cart. A low growl from Boots underscored the cat's growing irritation. Jenny had opted to take advantage of the PetSmart policy to bring her new friend shopping with her. She hated the thought of leaving the cat to do as he would upon the Mercedes' interior—especially since she'd just had the carpet steam cleaned.

"Your credit card," the cashier repeated and handed Jenny the MasterCard, "it's declining."

"Oh." Jenny dropped the rejected card into her smock pocket, scratched through her wallet, and pulled out another card. "Try this one then. Maybe there's a problem with the system or something." She eyed the bags of various cat goodies stacked in the cart. She'd spent nearly a hundred bucks on Boots. But he deserved it. This cat was going to be her best friend from now on.

The second Jenny had shed the box in the alley, Boots began romancing her with enough pitiful purring and yowls to melt the heart of a statue. She'd snatched him up and sprinted to the

Mercedes before his howling drew attention to her. When she'd pulled away from the curb, a last glance in the rearview mirror revealed Rothingham and his red-lipped vixen-of-a-daughter exiting the financial firm. He held a wadded cloth to his lip while Celia urged him toward the parking lot.

Jenny frowned and prayed she was never linked to that whole episode. An unexpected shiver attacked her, and she didn't even want to imagine the fallout of being discovered.

The cashier's nasal tone barged through Jenny's thoughts once more. Jenny focused on the Asian teenager in time to see her lips shape the word "Declined," although her voice seemed to be floating from a distant planet.

"What?" Jenny snapped and grabbed the card. She'd been using these two cards since she and Keith got married. He'd given them to her and told her to pay with them instead of cash or checks. He always took care of the bills at the end of the month and never asked for explanations. Likewise, Jenny never questioned Keith's ability to manage the money. She just left the whole thing to him and trusted that he wisely handled their finances. After all, he was a financial advisor who had a reputation for doing wonders with other people's money.

"There's something wrong somewhere," Jenny accused and eyed the computerized contraption posing as a cash register.

"Well, I'm sorry, Ma'am…" the cashier said with a helpless shrug.

Jenny noted her name was Candy and wondered if the girl was old enough to even be running a cash register. She didn't look more than twelve. Apparently the child was pressing a wrong button somewhere.

An annoyed parrot squawked nearby. Jenny jumped and glanced behind her. A father held a huge cage while his son gripped a small box from which the irate screeching erupted. Boots released a howl that would put goose bumps on a corpse. The father's exasperated glare suggested Jenny's turn at the checkout counter had expired.

"Okay...uh...just a minute," she mumbled and accepted the second credit card from the clerk. She pulled out a third, one she seldom used. Jenny held her breath while replacing both declined cards back into her billfold with as much nonchalance as she could feign.

The second the cash register began the wheeze and whir of finishing the transaction Jenny's spine relaxed. Glad the infant posing as a clerk had finally learned how to use the machinery, Jenny signed the slip and was out the door before the annoyed parrot and its new owner could complain much more.

The smells of pets and supplies were replaced with the whiff of car exhaust and warming pavement. Jenny whisked the cart across the parking lot and loaded Boots and his new stuff into the back of the car. After placing the cart in the rack, she sank into the driver's seat and, out of habit, took a peak in the vanity mirror. The hollow-eyed cleaning lady who peered back reminded Jenny of her wild morning. She looked like she didn't have a penny to her name. No wonder the clerk acted like it was her fault the cards were declined.

Her cell phone beeped from the dashboard, where Jenny had left it while it charged. *Must have missed a call*, she thought and checked the tiny screen. Sure enough, the "Missed Call" message was displayed on the screen. After she pressed the button to identify the caller, Jenny saw her husband's name displayed.

"Keith!" she hissed as her heart went cold. *What if Rothingham figured out it was me and called him, and now he's calling me?* Jenny dropped the phone like it was a viper loaded with venom. The cell clattered across the floor gearshift and clunked between her seat and the console.

Heaving for air, Jenny gripped the steering wheel and rested her forehead against it. She squeezed her eyes tight and swallowed the ocean of tears threatening to drown her. "Oh, God, please," she whispered, "if You'll just cover my tracks, I promise I won't ever sneak around like that again."

Boot's piteous meow escalated into a wail that sounded like something straight out of a Halloween horror movie.

"Okay, okay, kitty," Jenny croaked and lifted her head and rubbed at her moist eyes. "We're going home." She fumbled with the seat belt for what felt like thirty minutes before finally getting it to latch. By the time she inserted her key into the ignition and cranked the car, she decided to fish her cell phone from where it had fallen. Her fingers unsteady, Jenny turned the phone off. She couldn't talk to Keith right now. If he already knew about the invasion, she couldn't handle knowing he knew. If Keith didn't know, she feared he might suspect something was wrong by the tone of her voice.

After dropping the phone into the passenger seat and putting the car in reverse, Jenny decided to call Keith back later this afternoon. Once she'd gotten control of her emotions, she'd figure out how best to confront him about Celia Rothingham. She switched the gearshift to drive as the image of that Christmas photo blazed through her mind. Jenny's face flashed hot. She snapped on the air conditioner and adjusted the vent to blast her cheeks.

As another thought pummeled her brain, Jenny nudged the gas pedal with her foot. The car rolled forward. Keith insisted he was alone in Seattle. Jenny assumed he'd been adamant about being alone because he really wasn't. But he wasn't with Celia either. Celia was here in all her glory. Jenny slammed on her brakes, then checked her rearview mirror to see if someone was behind her. Fortunately the parking lot lane was all hers.

If Celia's here, does that mean he's involved with more than one woman? The question stomped through her heart and left a nauseous wake. Jenny rested her head against the headrest, closed her eyes, and knew she had to have some answers from Keith—and soon. She simply could not go on like this.

"So we're going to talk about wheat now, is that it?" Joe prodded with a chip-toothed grin. "No more of this Jenny business?"

"You *did* promise you'd tell all," Keith said and sipped his cappuccino. The coconut-flavored brew complemented the pastry to perfection.

"Okay. So I will, I will." Joe stood, turned the chair around, and dropped back into it. He leaned forward on his elbows and looked Keith squarely in the eyes. "The secret is," he began in a false conspiratorial voice, "the soil does most of the work once it's prepared right."

"As long as it takes its vitamins, you're in good shape. Right?"

"Well, we do have to pour the stuff into it, like I already said. We also have to know when to plant. The spring wheat is in April. The winter wheat, before the first freeze. For the winter crop, we have to stay in that window of time when the Hession fly and the whole Hession clan are on vacation—"

"Hession fly?" Keith found himself starting to get interested, despite the pending Jenny threat.

"Hession flies look at a wheat field like an all-you-can-eat buffet. We need to make sure we miss their fly date. We just cancel their reservations, and make sure they don't get a standby flight!" Joe wiggled his brows.

"Ha, ha," Keith said and felt like he'd swallowed a couple of Hession flies himself. His brain buzzed with all his problems, and he began to wonder if any of this was really going to alter his money issues.

"And don't forget the worms!" Joe added. He leaned back and rubbed the front of his sweatshirt like an old guy settling in for a long tale.

"How could I?" Keith shot back and recalled the summer his farming grandfather and he had cultured a huge bed of night crawlers. They were the best fishing bait ever. An unexpected longing for those simpler days nearly sucked Keith under. There were no bills. No profits and losses. No fatal failures. And no wife to face.

"The rain tills the soil near the surface," Joe continued, "while worms do the work further underground. Worms act like tiny plows, taking hard soil and crumbling it into fine bits. When we seed the ground, the soil takes over, unwrapping that seed and letting the miracle escape. The right soil makes all the difference." Joe nodded and gazed toward Lila, who had handled the customers and was putting on a fresh pot to brew. The door clanged open and a short, middle-aged woman bustled in. "Sorry I'm late," she said the second she spotted Lila. "I overslept."

"No prob, Saundra," Lila said as a trio of customers entered behind the newcomer.

Saundra hopped to the task, stepped behind the counter, and began her duties.

"Do you need to help them?" Keith asked.

Joe shook his head. "Nah. They'll do fine. They're a couple of troopers. If it gets too wild, I'll step in. But for now, I think they can handle it."

Keith tapped his fork against his empty plate. "So you're planting this spring?" he prompted before Joe had the chance to get back on the Jenny bandwagon.

"Yep. This spring. The time is really upon us. That's why Saundra's here. She helps me out when I need it."

"So, like, you're going to start planting *now*?"

Joe nodded. "Tomorrow, weather permitting. Wantta help?"

"Do I have a choice?" Keith dropped his fork on the saucer with a clank and clunk.

"Uh-uh." Joe shook his head. "Not as long as you're here. You need the lesson, and I need the hands. Marcy just told me she's got to work doubles all this week."

"So I need the lesson..." Keith leaned back and closed his eyes. He stretched his legs and imagined hours in the field, bent and weathered. "With all due respect, I'm still not making the connection between Hession flies and dirt vitamins and worms and my money problems."

"I never meant for you to."

Keith opened his eyes and didn't move. Once again he hoped Joe wasn't about to start some cultish spiel.

"All I wanted was to get you thinking about *your* soil."

"*My* soil?"

"Yep. The soil of your heart."

Keith lifted his brows.

"Inside each of us is 'ground,'" Joe drew invisible quotes in the air, "that needs planting. You know, with dreams, ambitions... desires. If the soil is fertile, our dreams'll grow. But if our soil is hard and untilled and has no nutrients, our dreams die and we fail."

Keith forgot to worry about the cult. He leaned forward, placed his elbows on the table, and stared at Joe. The guy looked as sane as ever. Furthermore, all this dirt business was starting to make sense.

"In so many words, you've said you want to get out of this fix you're in. Right?"

"Right." Keith nodded.

"Well, the soil of your heart has to be prepared or the seed of that desire will not be able to grow. There are some things you can do to find freedom, but you won't be able to pull them off until your soil is ready. Until then, you'll be stuck right where you are."

Joe crossed his arms, looked down, hesitated. "You know," he finally said, "sometimes the seed just rots in the ground."

Keith's face stiffened as cold dread seized him. He wasn't certain he understood all the implications of what Joe was saying, but he was grasping enough to know he was at a crossroad...and his decisions in the next few days would radically affect the future. He'd heard that during the Great Depression some had committed suicide when they lost their fortunes. While Keith had no plans for such, he understood the desperation—understood it all too well. He locked his clammy hands together and watched as the flames joyfully danced in the fireplace.

If only he could feel joy once more.

Joe's voice tugged his mind back to the present conversation.

"Marcy and I really struggled after I took over this place." Joe waved toward the coffee bar where Lila and Saundra were dashing around like two mice on a wheel of cheese. "I left a very good income at the ad agency, one that selling three-dollar cups of coffee didn't replace." He took a draw on his soda. "Lots of people think when you own a business you've got money coming out your ears. But if you're not careful, being self-employed can eat up every asset you ever thought about."

"Yeah…" Keith agreed and didn't bother to remind Joe he held a degree in finance. It was shameful enough to remember that fact without voicing it.

"At the time, Marcy was already stretched thin in her nursing job. I didn't want to ask her to work overtime. Given our personal financial obligations and the overhead of this place, we had some very lean months. I wondered if I was nuts to leave a good-paying job. Even though owning my own business had been a lifelong dream, I tell you, I went through a lot of tilling in my heart. Questions and doubts and more questions and worries." Joe shook his head and gazed past Keith as if a movie of memories were playing on a big screen behind him.

"It felt like those worms were working overtime. I thought all I had done was just a waste." Joe lifted both hands. "To be honest with you, it was the hardest time I have ever gone through." He wrapped his fingers around his glass.

"So what happened?" Keith asked and shoved his saucer to the side.

"Well, now I see that I had to go through those 'tilling times' for the soil of my heart to be ready for planting the seed of God's plan. The spiritual harvest has come since then. Just to tell you the truth, there were times when I didn't know how I'd make the next car payment. And, actually, it got so stressful, Marcy and I nearly went to split city."

"Really?" Keith asked.

Joe nodded. "Really."

"Well, you two didn't look like you were on the verge of splitting this morning, that's for sure."

"Nope. Not anymore." Joe's broad grin transcended any locker-room jock bragging but hinted of a marital bliss Keith and Jenny hadn't experienced in ages.

"But at that time, Marcy was working as hard as she could. I was working as hard as I could. We almost never saw each other. And it didn't seem like we were making any progress."

"So...you started eating worm dirt with vitamins," Keith quipped. "Is that it?" He picked up his napkin and tossed it aside.

Joe laughed out loud. "God *did* give me a few farming lessons," he admitted, "but, thankfully, we never had to eat dirt or worms."

"You guys need anything else?" Lila's cheerful voice announced her approach. She held a carafe of coffee and wore a knock-'em-dead smile.

"Oh sure," Keith agreed and pushed his cup toward her. "I started out with coconut cappuccino. Will this mix okay with that?"

"Yes. It's just the regular stuff. Nothin' fancy."

Joe smiled up at his employee. "Remind me to give Rick a tip," he teased.

"Rick? What for?"

"For suggesting I hire you."

"*I'm* the one who gets the tips!" Lila declared.

"Look both ways before you cross the street," Keith said.

"Good tip, man," Joe replied, and the two friends shared a high-five.

"You're impossible," Lila huffed. "I don't know how Marcy puts up with you."

"Oh, I'm much nicer to her than I am to you," Joe said with a nod.

"You better be," she shot back before meandering to another table.

"She's a good sport," Joe said.

"I guess it's a good thing." Keith stirred his coffee and enjoyed the hum and rhythm of the morning crowd's soft interaction. This place was like an old pair of slippers that felt good to come home to.

Finally he looked up at Joe and voiced the question he sensed his friend was awaiting. "Okay, so how do I...how do I, uh, prepare my soil?" He dragged the words out like a heavy chain and wondered if he was crazy for even asking. Keith knew from watching his grandfather that farming was nothing but back-breaking labor. Earlier this morning Joe had mentioned giving. Maybe that was what he was talking about. His grandfather had given his life to that farm, and it looked like Joe was doing the same. But by the same token, Joe never once suggested that Keith should take up farming. It seemed there was more going on here...much more. "So...what do I need to do?" he repeated.

"You've already done it, or should I say you're doing it now," Joe said. "You're talking about your failures. You're allowing the plow of truth to go in and cut beneath the surface and reveal the real issues."

"Yeah, and you don't know how much it hurts to be that honest."

"Oh yes I do," Joe assured him and scratched the back of his neck. "Been there. Done that. I think God is in the business of getting us to the place where we're so desperate we *have* to get gut-level honest."

"Ah, man." Keith cradled his face in his hands. "I *hate* this."

"Don't we all. It's tough to make changes. But if you'll look back over all the changes you've made in life, many times the ones that hurt the most are the ones that prepare you for something better in the future. The same applies to the things you're currently struggling with. I believe that…that, well, maybe God is asking you to change the way you view your life—money, marriage, gifts, the whole nine yards. You may not like what you're going through. It may feel like someone's tearing into your heart with a plow. But it is necessary."

Keith lifted his face.

"Just imagine if the soil could talk when it's being tilled."

"I don't have to imagine. I *know* what it would say." Keith balled his fists. "I'm torn to shreds and bleeding and confused."

"But don't you see? That's all part of the growth process." Joe's gaze grew intense. "We till the soil to prepare it for seed. It's the *tough* times that prepare us for growth and harvest." He leaned toward Keith, reached across the table, and grasped his shoulder. "You're in a time of soil-tilling right now. But that means the planting is just around the corner."

Chapter Nine

The next morning, Rick pulled his Ford pickup into Joe's winding driveway. The oak-lined lane leading to the log cabin reminded him of his folks' house in Oklahoma and all the summers he'd spent chasing garter snakes and rabbits as a kid. He'd barely turned off the ignition when he spotted the two men he'd come to visit in the back field. Rick tapped his thumb against the steering wheel and watched them work together.

Joe was driving a tractor, pulling a spreader that broadcast seed. After a long pass, he approached Keith, who used a wide, aluminum shovel to scoop seed from the bins into the spreader. Joe's German shepherd, his head and tail high, ran across the earth as if the planting couldn't happen without his presence. The spring air was enough to make the most lazy hound jump daisies.

The day was a for-sure winner when it came to planting. Rick gazed toward the blue sky. Early this morning a fine mist had threatened heavier rain, so he and Charlie had decided not to fish. Besides, Rick had endured another wild night with his granddaughter, and he didn't have the presence of mind to fight off Charlie's hooks. Despite it all, by 8:00 the mist had burned off and left nothing but clear blue skies and enough sunshine to melt a glacier.

Opening the truck door, Rick swung his legs out and slowly lowered himself to the ground. After pausing a minute to work out the arthritic kinks, he slammed the door and traipsed toward his friends. Rick fingered the hundred dollar bill in his pants pocket. The wave of peace that engulfed him confirmed he'd heard the heavenly prompting right.

Yesterday evening he was on the verge of giving a sizable cash gift to his daughter, Bev, when she mentioned a very important fact. Her husband, Buddy, was drinking heavily. From there, Rick put together a few details. Their financial problems were created because Buddy was spending money on liquor and gambling that he should be spending on rent and groceries. This morning Rick told his daughter that he'd help them when her husband sought some help first. Otherwise Rick figured he'd just be financing another drinking binge and more gambling.

Until Buddy got dry and sensible, Bev agreed she should stay with her parents. This meant Rick might not get a good night's sleep for many moons. His wide yawn stretched his lips past the comfort zone.

He thought about Keith's problems and knew they were of a different nature than Bev and Buddy's. Keith is a good kid. He's just had a bad turn lately. And it appeared that the Lord was interested in helping him out a bit and using Rick to facilitate it. Even though Rick knew a mere hundred bucks wouldn't come close to relieving Keith of his financial worries, maybe it would at least let him know that God hadn't forgotten him.

Rick joined Keith just as Joe was driving the tractor away to spread more seed.

Keith glanced toward Rick and smiled. "Hey, man," he greeted, then glanced toward Rick's truck, before the two pumped hands. "When did you get here? I didn't even hear you drive up."

"Just got here," Rick explained and clapped Keith on the shoulder like a father who's proud of his son. "I watched you and Joe work together a few 'fore I got out, though. Looks like Joe's planning for a good crop."

"Yeah, at least he's planting enough seed. I guess we'll see what happens, right?" Keith looked into Rick's eyes, then his gaze trailed to the mangled eyebrow.

"Oh, plenty'll happen, that's for sure." Rick touched his scar. "Has anyone told you how I got this baby?" he asked.

Keith's grin merged into a chuckle. "Uh, yeah. Joe told me yesterday. I guess Charlie's hooks are lethal."

For the first time Rick laughed about the whole incident. "I guess," he said and covered another yawn. "Charlie's a good guy… most the time."

"And how long have you two been fishing together?"

"Since Moses was born," Rick said.

"You were in Vietnam together, right?"

"Yes. I pulled Charlie out of a hole about five seconds before it exploded. I'd say he owes me, but he lost his fingers when he threw his body between me and a grenade." Rick rubbed his face. "I guess I shouldn't worry about an eyebrow, huh?"

Keith's smile ignited anew, and Rick was glad to see the kid grin—even if his eyebrow was the reason. At least something good was coming out of that fiasco.

"Joe said just a minute ago that we'd be taking a break soon. Why don't you join us? Marcy left enough chocolate chip cookies to make us happy for a really long time. There's plenty for you too."

"Ah, I would, but I need to get back home. Since I'm not fishing today, the wife's got a honey-do list a mile long. You know how that goes."

Keith's gaze faltered. "Yeah," he mumbled and nudged at a clump of earth with the toe of his boot.

Rick could have bitten off his tongue for having even uttered the word "wife," given the marital problems Keith had hinted about. *Best to just do what I came to do and get outta here before I permanently put my foot in my mouth,* he thought.

"Listen," Rick said and reached into his pocket. "I really came just to bring you this." He gripped Keith's hand and pressed the hundred dollar bill against his palm.

Blinking, Keith looked down and shook his head. "Rick! I never expected… You didn't have to… I can't take—"

Rick held up his hand. "Yes, you've got to take it. If you want to argue with someone, argue with the Lord. I'm just doing what He told me to do." With Keith sputtering protests, Rick hastened away. He had no intention of keeping that money, and he figured the quicker he got away the more likely Keith was to accept it.

Stunned, Keith gazed after Rick as he walked across the yard. Finally Keith began moving toward his friend. But the older man had already climbed into his truck and cranked it by the time Keith got out of the field. With a final salute, Rick turned the pickup around and drove away. Keith peered at the hundred dollar bill and wondered if Rick even had this much extra to give. He'd never barged into Rick's financial situation by any means, but he'd assumed that neither Charlie nor Rick were independently wealthy. And while a hundred dollar bill wouldn't begin to touch Keith's financial problems, he worried that perhaps Rick might be doing without some necessities to give it to him.

Keith unfolded the single bill and gazed at it until it blurred into a haze of green ink. He couldn't take it. He simply could not. He'd never taken handouts and wasn't going to start now.

"Whazzup?" Joe's voice merged into his thoughts, and Keith looked up to see him approaching.

He'd been so distracted by Rick's gift, he just now realized the tractor's rev and roar no longer hummed across the field. Keith simply lifted the hundred dollar bill. "Rick just came," he explained.

"He gave you this?" Joe exclaimed and snatched the money from Keith.

He nodded. "Yeah. But I can't take it."

"Yes!" Joe said, his face radiant. "You've *got* to!"

"But—"

"It's Rick's seed. And the whole thing won't work if you give it back."

"His seed?" Keith gazed toward the lane. The faint purr of Rick's pickup faded up the road.

"Yep. How would you feel if the ground spit the seed we'd planted back at us?"

"Uh…"

"Well, it's the same thing. This is exactly what I've been talking about the last couple of days." Joe lifted the hundred dollar bill toward the heavens and shouted, "Hallelujah!"

Keith scratched his head and decided he needed one of those

cookies…maybe two. This morning when he woke up, there was a ray of sunshine bathing the soil of his heart. Aside from the fact that he was starting to seriously worry about why Jenny wasn't returning his calls, Keith had felt good. Better than he had in weeks. He really hadn't known why; he just felt lighter. Somehow just knowing that there might be a hidden purpose for the struggles he was going through made it easier to face them. For the first time in months, he'd felt like there was a light at the end of the tunnel—and this time it wasn't from an oncoming train.

Now, Keith wasn't sure exactly how he felt. He'd enjoyed helping Joe plant. The basic act of getting his hands into a task…dirt under his nails, on his jeans…had been therapeutic. But this whole Rick thing had dashed aside all traces of triumph and left him bewildered. He couldn't take Rick's money. He just *couldn't. No matter what Joe says, the poor guy is a retired Vietnam vet, and—*

"Okay, I'm reading your mind like the morning news," Joe said. "You still don't get it, do you?"

"I…uh…"

"Come on." He grabbed Keith's arm and yanked him across the field.

Keith tripped and finally regained his balance. "You don't have to drag me," he groused and sneezed. Whatever Joe stirred up in the dirt was giving his nose all kinds of grief.

"Sorry." Joe released his grip and motioned Keith to follow.

When they stopped, they were at the seed bin on the edge of the field. Joe stuffed the hundred dollar bill into Keith's shirt pocket and thrust his hand into the mound of seed in the bin. He pulled up a handful, grabbed Keith's hand, turned it palm up and released half the seed. Keith's fingers curled around the tiny bits of life as some slipped through his fingers and whispered back into the bin.

Joe chose one seed, held it between his index finger and thumb, and allowed the rest to fall. "I never can get over how something so small can produce a stalk of wheat," he marveled. "Then we can make bread from the kernels on the stalk. These little guys reproduce themselves a thousandfold." He held the seed up and gazed at it with an awed expression only rivaled by that of a new father.

Keith gazed at the seeds pricking his palm and pondered Joe's comment. The seeds smelled of nature and the land and reminded Keith of Alabama sunshine and eating Popsicles on his grandpa's front porch. Since germination was so common, he'd never given it much thought—not even when he was a kid visiting the farm. But standing on the edge of this wheat field, he began to sense a fraction of the wonder Joe expressed.

"It *is* a miracle, isn't it?" he concurred.

"Absolutely," Joe affirmed. "When I first got started farming, I could hardly believe that those tiny seeds would amount to anything. But after the first year, I was convinced. A rich harvest is all packed into this tiny guy." He placed the seed in the center of his taut palm. "How it gets packed in there, I don't know. And I don't know how it gets out either! But I know that if I don't plant wheat seed, I won't harvest any wheat."

He looked Keith squarely in the eyes. "Comprende?"

"Uh, yeah." Keith stroked his shirt pocket. The hundred dollar bill crinkled against the fabric.

"And I know if I only plant a little bit of seed, only a few stalks of wheat will grow. The same thing applies when we plant alfalfa, or when Marcy tosses wildflower seeds out by the road." He motioned toward the lane. "We always get a harvest in proportion to what we sow."

"Okay…" Keith agreed.

"The same thing applies to money!" Joe snatched the hundred dollar bill out of Keith's pocket and waved it. "Or just about anything else in your life. If you don't sow seed, you won't reap a harvest."

Keith interrupted. "Money? How am I supposed to sow money? I don't have a bin full of money." He snatched the bill from Joe. "Right now this is just about all I have, and I'm not convinced I should keep *it!*"

"You've *got* to, man!" Joe bellowed, his face slowly matching his sandy red hair. "If you don't, you'll rob Rick of his harvest!"

Keith began to wonder if Joe might burst a blood vessel. "Why do you want to go and get so hyped?" Keith asked. "You're starting to show your Irish blood, here. Have some patience, will ya?" He dropped the handful of seed back into the bin. "I see what you're saying," he admitted. "It's just hard for me to think I should really do it, that's all." He eyed the stray seeds collected around the bin like tiny bugs languishing atop the dirt.

Joe covered his face and sighed. "Sorry I got so intense there," he said and rubbed the front of his soil-smeared work shirt. "I can see why you'd struggle with all this. After all, it's not exactly a concept that you can trace with a pen and paper, and you're a fact-finding kinda guy. I understand that. Look…why don't we go in for a while. Those chocolate chip cookies Marcy made last night are calling my name."

Stuffing the money into his jeans pocket, Keith nodded. "I feel your pain," he admitted while his cell phone released a series of short, shrill beeps. When he checked the phone's tiny screen, he noted the caller was his boss, Sinclair Rothingham. Keith drew his brows together and wondered what Mr. Rothingham could want.

"I'm sorry, Joe," he said, glancing toward his friend. "I'm going to have to take this one. It's my boss. Go on in. I'm sure I'll be there shortly."

Chapter Ten

"Heeeeeeeerrrrrrre kitty, kitty, kitty, kitty. Heeeeeeeerrrrrrre kitty, kitty, kitty." Jenny circled the maple while gazing up into the branches. She'd followed the piteous meows to the bushes near the tree. After searching the nearby shrubbery, Jenny had deduced that Boots must be hiding in the maple.

"Meow?"

Shivering against the cool Detroit air, Jenny wrapped her sweater tight and strained to spot a long tail, pointed ears, or golden eyes amid the fresh foliage.

"Meeeeooooooowwwwww!"

Movement on a lower limb caught her attention. The flash of soft fur on a black tail attested to Boots' presence. "There you are, you scoundrel," Jenny gently chastised. "What are you doing up there, you silly ol' cat?" Everything had been fine with Boots since Jenny brought him home yesterday. But this morning, when she opened the door to check the mail, he'd dashed past Jenny's legs and darted into the yard. Jenny had scrambled to catch him, but all she got was a scraped knee and scattered mail. She'd desperately searched for the cat for an hour, gave herself a long break, and then came back out about thirty minutes ago. When she was almost ready to accept that she'd lost her pet, Jenny'd heard a faint meow.

Now her quest had paid off. Boots peered down at her, his big eyes looking as hopeless as his voice sounded.

"You crazy cat," Jenny crooned. "Why did you want to go and escape?"

Boots kneaded the limb with his claws, half closed his eyes, and trilled out a purr-meow.

"I guess you've finally gotten hungry, haven't you?" Jenny said in a high-pitched voice. "Well, why don't you come on down, and I'll open a big can of that gourmet cat food I got for you. It's tuna," she enticed.

The cat blinked and crouched low on the limb.

"Now what?" Jenny mumbled and recalled the age-old scene of a fireman rescuing a kitten from a tree. But that was usually in smaller towns than Detroit…and closer to 1950 than the present. Jenny rested her hands on her hips and huffed. She couldn't even imagine calling the fire department. They'd probably laugh at her.

She thought about the ladder in the storage building behind the house and wished Keith were here. But he wasn't. He was in Seattle.

Jenny's eyes stung. She didn't even want to think about whether or not he really was alone. She'd cried herself to sleep last night. Then this morning she'd plastered on enough eye makeup to make a mummy look like Miss America. She hoped no one she happened to see noticed the puffiness.

Keith had called three times since yesterday, but Jenny hadn't answered. All three times he'd left a voice mail. This morning Jenny played and replayed the last message, in which he nearly begged her to return his call. She was on the verge of breaking down and calling when Boots escaped.

Sighing, Jenny hugged herself and rested her forehead against the tree. The bark pressing into her skin, she closed her eyes. All day yesterday she'd vacillated between wanting to whack Keith for going off like this and desperately wanting him back with no questions asked. All she knew was that he was not with Celia Rothingham. And who knew what happened between them around Christmas. If there was another woman besides Celia, Jenny was hard-pressed to figure out who. There were zero clues of other females in Keith's life.

Zero.

Sometime between last night's tears and being awakened this morning by Boots' cold nose on hers, Jenny had finally decided she wanted her man more than anything. With both her parents gone now, her relationship with Keith was her life. She could be the richest person in the world and it wouldn't matter without her husband. Plus, she'd so wanted to have a family one day…a trio of boys, all with Keith's dark hair and eyes.

"Oh dear God," Jenny prayed. "Please…please…*please*.…"

"Excuse me, Jenny?" a hauntingly familiar, male voice intruded upon her heavenly pleading.

Jenny jumped, stiffened, and dared not breathe.

I'm imagining things. I must be. The stress is making me wacky. Mr. Rothingham is not here. He can't be! Jenny cracked one eye and barely lifted her head. When the first glance confirmed her suspicions, she yelped, skittered back, and stared wide-eyed at her husband's boss. Her frantic gaze darted toward his Cadillac in the driveway, then back to the tall patriarch.

"Excuse me," he began again. "I didn't mean to—"

"Mr. Rothingham!" she gasped and dug her fingers against the top of her sweater. She looked up all six feet of him and into the pale, blue eyes and rigid face she'd gazed into yesterday. Except today his lower lip protruded out in a red bulge, and a neat row of stitches marred the tissue. He wore a gray suit and white shirt that made him look more like a pallbearer than a financial executive.

In a whirl of crazy thoughts, Jenny was certain he'd figured out she was the one he'd chased from the office yesterday. Perhaps he'd come to drag her to the police station.

"Are you okay?" Mr. Rothingham asked and moved in to touch Jenny's arm. "You look very pale."

Jenny jerked back. "I…I…I…" she garbled and couldn't find a thing to say. Her legs shook so violently she leaned against the tree to stop herself from collapsing.

"Meow!" Boots wailed, and Rothingham glanced upward.

"It's my—my cat," Jenny stuttered. As soon as the words left her mouth, Jenny feared she'd made a horrible mistake in acknowledging the creature. If Rothingham recognized Boots from the alley, that might be all he needed to confirm her as the prowler.

"That's nice," he said and dismissed the feline in preference for scrutinizing her.

Jenny gulped.

"I just called Keith a few minutes ago," he explained. "He asked me to come check on you. He's very worried about you. He says he's tried to call and isn't getting an answer." His smile held an odd curiosity that looked like a leopard wondering what the gazelle he'd cornered was going to taste like.

"Uh…" Jenny clenched and unclenched her fist. "Um…" She

licked her lips and wondered why Mr. Rothingham had called Keith. It could have been routine business. Or he could have been asking Keith why his wife had broken into the firm.

"I was just about—about to call him, act–actually," she babbled and cleared her throat.

"Good." He nodded. "He's really worried that you're not okay. Just so you know," he gazed toward the massive brick home, then back to Jenny, "we had a prowler at the office yesterday."

"Really?" Jenny bleated. She leaned harder against the tree and pressed her fingers into the bark until it pricked beneath her nubby fingernails like needles.

Rothingham nodded. His face settled into a stern angle that accented the lines around his mouth. "Yes. I called Keith to tell him. Somehow a woman got in without any signs of breaking and entering."

"Really?" Jenny repeated.

"Yes." He gazed past Jenny and narrowed his eyes. "I saw her, and I'd know her in a heartbeat if I ever saw her again."

"You would?"

"You bet I would," he snarled. "She's the reason my lip is busted and I've got hot tea burns all over my chest. I'd just gotten the cup out of the microwave. And I'll never forget her face again as long as I live."

Jenny clutched her throat and was certain he was about to drag her by the hair all the way to jail.

"Mr. Rothingham…" she pleaded.

His gaze snapped back to Jenny. His face softened. "Oh," he quietly asserted, "you look terrified. Did I scare you?" He reached for her hand. "I'm sorry." Rothingham's smile never had seemed sincere to Jenny. His present attempts did nothing to change her opinion.

Nevertheless, a slow realization began to seep through her terror. Rothingham had no idea she'd been the intruder. None. Her disguise had worked. She shifted from her dependence on the tree as he released her fingers.

"That's the reason I called Keith," he explained, "to let him know about the prowler. We're re-keying the firm and having new locks placed on all our office doors. The doors already had locks on them, but everyone of us had gotten slack about keeping them locked. In fact, we've even forgotten to set the alarm a few times. We've started a new policy now. All offices must be locked and the alarm set when we leave."

"I see," Jenny breathed. "Did this woman take anything…" Her mind whirled with what to say next, "…from Keith's office?" she continued, and decided that was a good choice. Made her sound nice and uninformed and naturally concerned about her husband.

"No." He shook his head. "We can't see that anything is missing. She was obviously after something in Celia's office, but the only damage done was that she royally messed up a drawer of Celia's papers. There is a chance she might have been looking to steal one of our identities. That's all the rage now, you know."

"Yes." Jenny swallowed. "Yes, I know."

"I'm suggesting that all our employees change their credit and debit card numbers. Might not be a bad idea for you too. It never hurts to be safe."

A giddy giggle, laced with relief, threatened to totter from Jenny. She pressed her fingertips against her lips and looked down.

"Look, I know this is terribly disturbing," Rothingham soothed.

"Yes, terribly," Jenny mumbled past her fingers and swallowed.

"But I really think everything's going to be fine. And I know Keith will be glad to hear you're okay. He was really worried—especially after I told him about the prowler. He was afraid maybe someone got his address from his office and had done something to you."

All vestiges of hilarity were swept aside in the face of surprise and hope. "He was really worried?" Jenny asked and searched Rothingham's face.

"Sure." The man's mouth flexed into gentle mockery. "Why wouldn't he be? You're his wife."

She diverted her gaze.

"Jenny…" he hesitated, "look, I don't know what's going on here, but I hope you understand that we really like you and Keith. He's a hard worker. So are you. *Both* of you have helped us land some *great* clients."

Glancing up, Jenny rubbed the top of her thumbnail, rough from the sculptured nail. Even though he still wasn't at the top of her favorites list, Rothingham looked sincere enough…for once.

"Whatever's up, I hope the two of you will…" He shrugged.

"Thanks," she rasped.

Keith sat on Joe's porch swing, gazing toward the freshly planted earth. In one hand he held an empty water bottle. In the other, the last bite of one of Marcy's chocolate chip cookies. The treats were so full of nuts and chocolate they had to be worth ten bucks apiece. Keith popped the final bite in his mouth and savored the morsel. The late morning sun bathed the land in silvery warmth that Keith wished could penetrate his soul.

After the conversation with Mr. Rothingham, Keith had been engulfed with dread. Whoever that invader was, he hoped she hadn't somehow gotten to Jenny. He checked his cell phone for the third time in as many minutes. Mr. Rothingham promised he'd go by and check on Jenny himself, but that had been an hour ago. He'd had ample time by now. If Jenny didn't call in a few more minutes, Keith would try to call her again. If he didn't reach her, he would call Mr. R one more time.

He set the bottle on the handrail, hunched forward, stared at the phone, and willed it to ring. It remained silent.

The front door rattled and Joe appeared, dressed in a fresh pair of jeans and a polo shirt that read "Mac's Place" across the front. "Okay, I'm outta here," he chimed. Joe banged the door shut and hurried across the porch. "Sure you don't want to come with me?" he shot toward Keith.

"Yeah," Keith mumbled and straightened. Nevertheless, he couldn't pull the slump from his shoulders. Joe had received the phone call halfway through the cookie experience. Seemed one of the coffee machines was on the fritz this time.

"I don't normally go back and forth like this, but it looks like it's just one of those weeks. I shouldn't be gone long."

"Okay," Keith said and tried to smile. "Tell Lila I said hello."

"Will do." Joe waved and trotted down the steps like he had the world by the tail. During their cookie-devouring session, Joe had backed off his soil-preparation, seed-sowing soliloquy. Instead, he'd talked about his latest fishing trip and asked Keith if he'd like to try his hand. Keith hadn't committed—not that the whole idea didn't sound good—but he really didn't know how much longer he should stay in Seattle. He'd told Mr. Rothingham he'd be back in a week. Keith had already spent two nights in Washington, and he knew Jenny well enough to figure she was imagining all sorts of scenarios.

The whole business with Jenny so loomed over him that Keith had been thankful Joe got the call about the coffeemaker. Keith welcomed the time alone. He had a lot to think about...like whether or not Jenny was okay...how in the world he was going to tell her that he'd lost her inheritance...and whether or not Joe's seed theories were hypothetical wishing that might or might not work.

Keith eyed the cell phone. He felt like a teenage kid waiting for "the girl" to return his call. But this time "the girl" just happened to be his wife, and the worries were multiplying by the second.

"Come on, Jenny," he muttered seconds before his phone began the familiar beep that signified her call.

Keith looked at the screen and noted Jenny's cell number displayed there. He moved his thumb to the answer button and hesitated. Now that she'd called, Keith wasn't sure exactly what to say. He pressed the button and held the phone to his ear.

An urgent "Psssttt!" pulled Keith's attention toward the right, and Joe was retracing his steps from the driveway. "Is that Jenny?" he whispered and paused on the other side of the handrail.

"Hello, Jenny?" Keith said into the mouthpiece and nodded at Joe.

"Hi, Keith." Jenny's hesitant voice sounded as if she were halfway around the world.

"Tell her!" Joe urgently mouthed. "You've *got* to tell her!"

Chapter Eleven

By some miracle of Mother Nature, Jenny had managed to coax Boots out of the tree after Mr. Rothingham left. Of course, the can of real tuna hadn't hurt her mission. Boots, driven by the call of his stomach, had delicately climbed down the tree until Jenny was able to pull him into her arms. He'd eaten his tuna, licked his paws in royal order, and curled up on the settee for a nice nap after his traumatic morning.

Now Jenny held her cell phone in one hand and stroked Boots with the other. The phone trembled against her ear as severely as her fingers shook atop Boots' fur. She swallowed hard and reminded herself that this *was* her husband—the man she was supposed to know better than anyone else in the world. But lately she felt like she'd never known him at all.

"Jenny?" Keith said.

"Yes." She closed her eyes and rested her head against the back of the velvet settee.

"Are you all right?"

"Yes, I'm fine," she said.

"I asked Mr. Rothingham to check on you."

"He did."

"I was worried."

"That's nice to know," Jenny said and couldn't stop the barb in her tone. She raised her head and opened her eyes.

"Jenny..."

"You ran off to Seattle without even telling me, and *you're* worried?" Jenny stood and paced toward the fireplace.

Silence floated over the line.

"Where are you, anyway?" Her fingers tightened on the phone. She never intended this conversation to take such a turn. Some part of her really wanted to beg Keith to just come back home. But her pent-up frustration was taking over, and everything was coming out all fast and all wrong.

"I'm at Joe and Marcy Conrad's place. Joe owns Mac's Place in downtown Seattle. Remember? They have a small farm in Ellensburg now."

Jenny closed her eyes and recalled her first date with Keith...if you could call it a date. He'd asked her to meet him for coffee on Saturday morning at some out-of-the-way coffee shop. Jenny had felt as if she were stepping into a safe haven, and Keith's easy smile and kind eyes insisted *he* was as safe a haven as the shop. Jenny vowed he'd stolen her heart over a cup of cappuccino and a croissant that was covered in coconut and stuffed with some cream that was so good it should be outlawed.

"Of course I remember," Jenny replied, her voice several decibels lower. She opened her eyes and dug her sock-clad toes into the plush carpet. "When we got married Joe and Marcy gave us that basketful of coffee that took nearly a year to use up."

"Yeah," Keith said. "Uh...and Jenny?" he added.

"Yes."

"I *really am* alone." His sincere tone left no room for doubt.

"Okay," Jenny said and swallowed. *But what about you and Celia and the Santa picture?* she thought but didn't voice it—mainly because she'd have to explain how she saw the photo in the first place.

"I really wish you wouldn't worry about me like that," Keith said, a defensive edge to his voice.

"Well, when you leave town without telling me—what exactly do you expect me to think?" she snapped. "How would you feel if I left one day for work, and you found out I flew to Seattle instead?"

More silence.

Boots lifted his head and released a faint meow.

While her mind whirled with thoughts and worries and all manner of "what if's," Jenny marched from the living room toward the sunroom and stopped at the patio door. She yanked on the drape cord, and the curtains swished aside to reveal the massive backyard. A primal urge suggested Jenny should throw the cell phone into the pool and follow that with the potted plants strategically placed around the deck.

"I'm sorry," Keith finally said.

Jenny rested her forehead against the cool glass. "Keith, what is going on?"

"I...Jenny, I...I just need some time away right now."

"*Keith, what's the matter?*" Jenny insisted. "Whatever it is, we can work through this together. Even if there is another woman," she begged, "I just want my marriage back."

"Blast it, Jenny! There's no woman! There never has been. It's only you."

That Santa–Celia photo hopped through Jenny's mind again. Either Keith was lying or he was a victim of Celia's aggressive nature. Jenny pondered the possibility that his surprised look could have been shock at Celia's presence, not at getting caught.

Something inside Jenny wanted to believe her man more than she'd ever believed in him before. But even in the face of this desire, she also sensed he was hiding something from her. Something was wrong. And he wasn't telling her.

"Well," Jenny finally croaked, "I know *something's* wrong. I don't know what it is, but I know." She waited for Keith to finally come clean. His continued silence was her only answer.

A fresh tide of frustration surged through Jenny. She'd *thought* their marriage was based on honesty and that Keith respected her enough to share his problems. "When you get ready to tell me what's going on, you know my number," she snapped. "Until then, don't bother calling." Her teeth clenched, Jenny pressed the cell's "end" button and threw the phone across the room. It crashed into the open-faced curio claiming the corner and shattered a set of crystal goblets she and Keith hadn't used since their wedding.

Keith pulled the phone away from his ear and looked at the screen. "Call ended" claimed the center. His face felt as cold as his heart. He didn't look toward Joe, but he still felt his presence. His unspoken question of "Why didn't you tell her?" was every bit as tangible as the man who thought it.

"Because I'm a coward," Keith answered and looked his friend in the eyes. "I'm a loser *and* a coward," he ground out.

"You aren't a loser," Joe insisted. "You aren't!" He grabbed the handrail. "You just made a few wrong moves. We've all done that. And I'm sure if Jenny is half the woman you've told me she is, she'll be there for you, and the two of you can move forward together."

"I think it's easier to just disappear." Keith wondered why Joe's farm hadn't opened up and swallowed him alive today. That seemed so much simpler than this mass of complications he'd created. And presently he didn't see how in the world Joe thought his simple solutions would make a bit of difference in his life. While Keith understood the guy was trying to help, his answers were far from practical.

"You know," Joe mused, "some of what I told you today out in the field works with marriage too."

"I need some time alone," Keith said and stood. He couldn't take another syllable of Joe's platitudes. Not one. Keith knew he was behaving rudely to one of his best friends, but he couldn't stop the abrupt way he headed for the door or the angry bang of the front door as he whipped it shut behind him.

Rick slumped in his corner chair at Mac's Place. His lids heavy, he allowed his mind to drift from worries about his daughter to whether or not he should ask for a refill on his decaf. He wondered about the Keith-man and his issues. Finally his mind wandered down a path that was heavy with fog…comfortable and inviting. Rick succumbed to the mist. His eyes closed and didn't reopen. The fog immersed him. He drank of slumber and relished the essence of relaxation.

A scrape and thump jolted him from the gauzy comfort. He jumped straight up, flailed his arms, and stiffened. In a whirl of confusion, Rick didn't know whether he should expect shrapnel or his granddaughter's shriek.

"Oh, man," Joe said, "I didn't know you were snoozing. Sorry." He plopped into the chair across from Rick, rested his elbows on the table, and rubbed his heavy face.

"Whazzup?" Rick yawned. He'd give his life's savings for just three hours sleep...all at one time in one place.

"Gotta problem," Joe said and eyed Rick's cooling brew. "Need a refill?"

"Nah. I'm all coffee'd out." Rick looked into the mug, swirled the liquid, took a tiny sip, and wrinkled his nose. "Stuff's *awful* cold." He yawned again. "So what gives?"

"I've been telling Keith about the soil and planting business—everything you told me—and I just don't think he's getting it." Joe slumped back in his chair and fiddled with the corner of Rick's paper napkin.

Rick chuckled. "Yeah...I wondered if you were going to get it too," he admitted. "I remember thinking you were the most thick-skulled white man I'd ever met."

"Humph. And I guess no black man's ever been thick-skulled?" Joe teased.

"Absolutely not!" Rick said through a broad grin. "*I* certainly never have been."

"I bet Charlie's got another opinion on that."

"Why'd you have to bring Charlie into this?" Rick questioned.

"Ah, you love him," Joe asserted.

"Yeah, I guess so," Rick admitted through a yawn. "But don't tell him I said that, okay?"

"Humph. Listen, thanks for what you did for Keith today," Joe said with a genuine light in his eyes. "And you drove all the way to Ellensburg just to do it. I'm impressed."

Rick examined his palms, much softer now than they'd been in his youth. "Gave me something to do. Besides, you drive back and forth all the time like it's nothing."

"Well, I'm used to it."

"I just did what I felt like I needed to do. I didn't know if you were talking to Keith today about the sowing and reaping business, but I figured it wouldn't hurt to have a real-life example if you were. If you weren't, I still did what I was supposed to do." He tugged on the end of his beard and figured he was in for a trim. "I've been close to where he is a time or two. It's hard. A hundred dollar bill from a friend means a lot."

The door creaked open. The bell jangled. Charlie marched into the room like a short, scrawny general seizing new territory.

"Speak of the devil." Rick lifted his hand and smiled toward his best friend.

"Hey!" Charlie called and waved toward Lila, busy behind the counter. "I'll have the usual," he called.

"Right, Sir Charles," she replied with a smirk.

Charlie grimaced and glared at Rick, never once breaking stride. "Are you the one who taught her to be so sassy?" he demanded as he plopped into the vacant chair between Rick and Joe.

"Absolutely not," Rick claimed. "She got it all from her mother. That sister of mine is as feisty as they come. And I feel sorry for her husband, even to this day." He rubbed his face hard and stretched his eyes. "Man, I'm sleepy. I'm 'bout ready to check into a hotel for a night or two, just to get some sleep."

"You can come to my place," Charlie offered as he rolled up the sleeves of his worn, plaid shirt. "I'm sure Li would wait on you hand and foot and spoil you rotten."

"Sounds like an offer I can't refuse," Rick said. "The only person my wife's interested in spoiling rotten these days is Leandra."

"Ah, poor baby," Charlie crooned and patted Rick's shoulder.

"Get your hands off me," Rick snapped and pushed at Charlie's hand.

Joe laughed out loud. "You two slay me."

Lila showed up with a coffee carafe in one hand and a tall cola in the other. She set the cola in front of Charlie, extended the pot toward her uncle, and refilled his mug before he could stop her. "You look like you need a double, Uncle Rick," she said.

He eyed the steam leaping off the top of the dark liquid and didn't think a quadruple hit of caffeine would jolt him out of the stupor. He was too old for all this baby business. End of discussion.

"Thanks," Rick mumbled and sipped the hot liquid, despite his rejection of Joe's previous offer.

"And what'll you have, Boss?" she questioned.

"I'll have what Charlie's got," he said and glanced across the room. A dozen tables were occupied by one or two people each. "If you have time," he added.

"Sure," Lila said. "Anything for you. You just saved me from that coffee maker demon." She fondly punched him in the arm and swiveled toward the counter.

"She's a good kid," Rick said. "I raised her well."

"And if she'd turned out wilder than a March hare, you'd have blamed your sister, right?" Charlie chided.

"Absolutely!" Rick leaned forward and joined in the laughter.

"Hey, where's Keith?" Charlie asked and gazed around the room while sliding his three-fingered hand up and down the soda.

"I left him at my place." Joe picked up the napkin and tore the edge.

"He's been trying to talk to Keith about the Cycle of Giving," Rick explained. "And the boy's not catching on any faster than Joe did." He snickered. "I think it's Divine justice, myself."

"Well, I've got an idea." Charlie eagerly leaned toward Joe. "I was going to mention it to you today anyway. Maybe this is the answer to the problem."

"Oh?" Joe shifted in his chair. His gloom and doom expression lightened a bit.

"Why don't you bring him out to Li's Place?"

Narrowing his eyes, Joe glanced toward Rick. "Bamboo!" Rick blurted. "It's Charlie's cure for everything—global warming, warts, and peace on earth."

"*Come on*," Charlie said, his ruddy skin growing redder. "I'm dead serious here. You know, Joe. Li showed you everything a few years ago. Remember?"

Joe's eyes rounded. He sat straighter in his chair. "Yes, I remember. Of course." Ramming the heel of his hand against his forehead, he said, "How could I have forgotten?"

Rick narrowed his eyes and, for the first time, suspected that he might have been missing something. Charlie married Li Tang just over a year ago, after being a widower for nearly five years. The two acted like teenage sweethearts most the time, and Charlie thought everything Li did was beyond miraculous. Rick hadn't given her bamboo greenhouse much thought other than the times when Charlie brought it up. But now he wondered if maybe he'd been mistaken in his skepticism.

"Have you seen Li's shop, Rick?" Joe asked.

"Well, yeah, but—"

"But nobody's given Rick the lowdown," Charlie asserted. "And it's high time."

"Okay, okay, I'll come," Rick said and raised his hands, "but only if I get a nap after whatever it is I'm coming to see."

"Deal!" Charlie said.

Chapter Twelve

The next morning Keith pressed his face against the living room picture window. Rain pelted the glass and trickled down in tiny rivulets that did nothing to lift his spirits. The glass felt cool to his skin…nearly as cool as his heart. He eyed the field where they planted wheat the day before. The earth looked as barren as his life. No promises. No green.

Yesterday Joe had stayed in Seattle until Mac's Place closed at 8:00. Marcy came home mid-afternoon, looking like she'd worked 48 hours straight. She'd gone straight to her bedroom and crashed. After several hours of TV, Keith fixed himself a sandwich and holed up in his room. Sometime before the late news, Joe stuck his head in the room and asked Keith if he was up to a field trip the next day. Keith had agreed.

Despite his messed-up sleeping schedule and the time difference, he'd slept later this morning. When he awoke at 7:00, Keith felt as alone as he had last night. He'd debated whether or not to call Jenny, but every time he considered the option, he could hear Joe whispering, "Tell her." And that was something Keith still couldn't muster the will to do. Looking for peace, Keith finally tried to pray. But once the "Dear God" was spoken, all he could think about was the soil and the seed and the wheat. And that was exactly what consumed him now. Despite his mind's insistence that Joe's Cycle of Giving was in no way logical, another side of him suggested it was the only way to live.

"See any sprouts?" Joe's cheerful voice boomed from behind.

"Oh hey, man." Keith glanced over his shoulder. "I didn't hear you come in." He wiped at his chilled forehead and gazed back toward the field. "It hasn't grown one bit," he said. "With all this rain you'd think it would be at least a foot tall already."

Joe laughed. "Yep. A time or two I've been tempted to see if I could help it and pull the sprout on out of the ground. But all that does is mess up the whole process." Joe meandered toward the front door. "Ready for our field trip?" he asked, his eyes as eager as a kid's the first day of summer.

"Uh, yeah," Keith agreed and followed Joe. "But what about breakfast?" he rubbed his grumbling gut and peered toward the open kitchen.

"We'll grab something at a drive-through," Joe said and reached for a pair of jackets hanging on hooks near the door. Keith slipped into a worn, denim coat that looked as comfortable as his borrowed jeans felt. He was getting as used to the boots as he was to the jeans and work shirt.

Soon they were settled in Joe's cluttered farm truck and driving through rain that slowed to a drizzle the closer they got to Seattle. Joe finally stopped at a drive-through and passed Keith a sausage biscuit and a Styrofoam cup of coffee. The entrée was about as inviting as a leftover dog biscuit, and the coffee tasted like somebody had recycled yesterday's brew. This morning when he got up, Keith had "farmer's breakfast" on the brain. He hid his lack of enthusiasm and wondered how long it would be before he couldn't afford even a rubbery sausage biscuit and bad coffee.

Once they drove back on the highway, Keith's curiosity got the best of him. "Where are we headed, anyway? Are we going for more seed? Maybe a new shovel—since I just about wore that one out." He drained the last dregs of his coffee and winced. "I know—you're going to buy more acreage somewhere. You said it was a 'field trip.'"

Joe grimaced and shot Keith a harried glance. "Your jokes are getting worse than Charlie and Rick's."

"Ugh!" Keith gripped his chest. "You got me."

Laughing, Joe said, "No farms today. We did the farm thing yesterday. That field is finished. Now we wait." He exited off the freeway.

"That's the hard thing, isn't it? Waiting. How long after you plant wheat do you have to wait for something to happen?" Keith gazed toward the Cascade Mountains on the horizon and wondered how long they'd been there exactly as they were.

Joe slowed the truck near a driveway on the outskirts of Seattle. A large parking lot surrounded an Asian-looking greenhouse with an attached gift shop. The sign on the front of the store read "Li's Place: Bamboo Nursery Gardens." He maneuvered the truck into the parking lot and found a space near the front door.

Finally Joe turned to Keith. The look in his eyes revealed certainty mixed with a bit of frustration that Keith suspected he was the cause of. He hadn't exactly been the most stellar student.

"Believe me, something is happening with the seed right now," Joe answered. "The minute you plant, stuff starts happening, even if you can't see it." He looked toward the nursery and turned off the engine. "Just like it does in our lives," he said, but the claim was so soft it sounded more like an echo than a proclamation.

"I guess I haven't been the best learner, have I?" Keith admitted and shifted in his seat.

"Why would you say that?" Joe's chipped-tooth grin held an edge.

"I'm driving you crazy, aren't I?"

"Well, I…" Joe's wool jacket moved with his shrug.

"Sorry I stomped off on you yesterday." Keith tapped the arm-rest.

Joe's punch in Keith's arm was swift and firm. "No harm done. Look, there's somebody I want you to meet. You know Charlie got married last year."

"No!" Keith bellowed. "Why didn't you *tell* me?"

"I have no idea," Joe replied. "I'm telling you now. Does that count?"

"I guess so," Keith said through a chuckle.

"Anyway, his wife owns this place." Joe gestured toward the greenhouse. "Her name's Li Tang Sawyer. She's very interesting. I want you to meet her."

"Okay. Sure," Keith said and wondered what this had to do with anything. But, oh well, he'd come to Joe for help and the guy *was* trying.

They entered the nursery's retail store. The smells of live greenery and soil tinged with cinnamon welcomed Keith, and he felt some of his tension drain as he gazed across the shop. It was filled with plain and decorative clay pots, each with bamboo plants varying in height from less than a foot to those that scraped the ceiling. Keith wandered around looking at the plants, admiring their beautiful leaves and strong stalks. After a few minutes, Joe approached him accompanied by a woman who had a smile that Keith figured grabbed Charlie at first glance. Not far behind, Charlie and Rick trailed after her. As usual, they were a fishing trip waiting to happen. Both wore fishing vests. Rick held his lucky bass hat. Charlie had on a T-shirt that said, "My fish is bigger than yours."

"Keith, I'd like you to meet Li Tang Sawyer," Joe said, "the world's greatest expert on bamboo. She has forgotten more about bamboo than most people ever learn."

The attractive Asian woman, who looked to be in her fifties, shook hands with Keith and said with a heavy Texas drawl, "Joe never meets a hyperbole he doesn't like."

Keith smothered a chortle. This lady apparently did *not* grow up in Asia.

"It's nice to meet you, Keith," she said and reached for Charlie's arm. "Welcome to our nursery. All we grow is bamboo. But with such a versatile plant, why grow anything else?"

Charlie beamed like he'd won the hand of Miss America. "Can you believe I married her?" he bragged.

"I'll agree she's way too good for you," Rick chided.

"Of course she is," Charlie admitted. "That's why I married her. Think I'd marry a woman who wasn't good enough for me?"

The whole group laughed.

Li was all of five feet tall with auburn hair that undoubtedly came out of a bottle but still nicely suited her. Her dark eyes were set behind silver-framed glasses, and a silver panda earring adorned each earlobe. She wore a Hawaiian-print dress that was perfect with her animated features. Her wide smile revealed one gold tooth that seemed to rise from a sea of pearly white.

"I met Li when she came into Mac's Place for tea one day," Joe explained.

"Cinnamon." Li nodded and gazed at Charlie. "I'll never forget it."

"I was there," Charlie explained. "She dropped the tea. I helped her pick it up and asked her to marry me before we stood."

Joe's mellow voice confirmed the tale. "That's pretty close to the truth—as long as you don't count the two-year courtship."

"Well, I think it's all great. Just great," Keith said and recalled the days when Jenny's face had glowed with the same respect and adoration Li exhibited for Charlie. He nearly groaned out loud. If Jenny walked out on him over all this money business, he didn't know what he'd do. Granted, they'd fought like a couple of tigers in the last few months, but his wife was still his treasure.

Yes, and you need to tell her that. The thought was so strong, Keith looked to see if Joe had spoken it. He never noticed Keith's glance. Keith looked down. The tips of his work boots were worn. The jeans were torn. But in some strange way, he was feeling freer than he had in months. The suit and all it represented was swiftly losing appeal.

What was I thinking when I took such a big gamble? he fretted. The high-risk stock had promised quick and speedy returns. He'd taken similar risks for brave clients who approved the venture and doubled their money within a year. Keith had been sure the same scenario would befall him. He couldn't lose. He never had. He'd imagined himself coming home to Jenny with his monetary trophy and being a bigger hero in her eyes than ever.

But I fell flat on my face, he thought and shoved his hands deep into the jeans pockets.

"Li's taught me a lot about bamboo and all sorts of other things," Charlie's claim pierced Keith's thoughts.

He glanced up to notice Rick's hungry gaze scouring the place. The poor guy had bags under his eyes, and Keith remembered Joe's mentioning something about his daughter and her baby moving in.

"Li," Joe's voice held a hesitant edge, "I think Keith needs a lesson in bamboo."

So this is our field trip, Keith thought. *We've gone from wheat to bamboo.*

"Look," Charlie said, "Rick and I are going to make ourselves scarce, okay?" He kissed Li's cheek. "I'm going to give him the tour."

"Wonderful," Li said and tilted her head back to gaze up at Rick. "You'll be fishing with a bamboo pole by this time tomorrow," she prophesied and pointed at him.

Rick smiled. "Do I have a choice?"

The whole group burst into laughter, and Charlie motioned Rick toward the greenhouse.

Li led Keith and Joe through the jungle of potted plants into a small office that was as neat as Joe's truck was cluttered. By the time the door closed, Keith was engulfed in the cinnamon scent that teased his senses when he entered the shop. While he'd never been a huge fan of warm tea, the steaming urn on the brass stand in the corner offered way more promise than the road-kill coffee he'd drank. The bitter taste had yet to leave his tongue.

"Tea?" Li asked politely.

"Sure!" her guests answered in unison and found seats in the corners of the love seat.

While Li poured the dark liquid from an exquisitely painted teapot into delicate cups with equally delicate saucers, Keith glanced around the office. On one wall hung a set of ornate oriental fans. On the other hung a picture of a herd of Texas longhorns. A University of Texas cup sat on her desk. A detailed Persian rug covered the wooden floor. He smiled to himself and figured she and Charlie had some very interesting discussions during college football season. Charlie despised the Texas Longhorns.

Li arrived in front of them with two cups full of steaming liquid that promised to rid Keith of the bitter tongue syndrome. He accepted his cup and faced a major dilemma. Hard pressed to get his finger through the tea cup's handle, he finally just gripped it lightly around the top before taking a gingerly sip. The cinnamon chased away all traces of bitterness. Even though sipping cinnamon tea from china cups wasn't his normal forte, Keith went for another sip and relished the warmth.

"This is the way it's done," Joe teased and lifted one pinky before slurping the tea like a sow.

After playfully slapping at his arm, Li said, "Keith, this guy's gonna teach you all sorts of bad manners."

Chapter Thirteen

Li served herself some tea and settled into the wicker chair opposite them. She looked directly at Keith. "Joe said you were facin' some challenges."

So much for chitchat, Keith thought and didn't think he ought to glance away. Li's glasses magnified her eyes and made her look like she could stare down a freight train.

"He really didn't say much," she continued and paused for a swallow. "Maybe you're starting a new business. And maybe you're like Joe was—trying to keep the lights on and the coffee brewing at the same time."

Wondering exactly what all Joe had told her, Keith darted a gaze toward his friend, whose rapt attention rested on Li.

"When I first met Joe, he told me he was having a little trouble making ends meet—like sittin' on a barbed-wire fence with fortune on one side and bankruptcy on the other." The auburn-haired lady smiled even wider, her eyes sparkling.

Joe laughed sheepishly. He set his tea cup on the glass-topped coffee table and began slipping off his jacket. "When I first met Li," he explained, "I had been owner of Mac's Place for just a few months. I'd been successful in the advertising world, and just figured I'd be successful in the coffee shop business too. I hadn't counted on the learning curve."

"Or the fact that you are the poster child for a condition called acute impatience," Li teased.

"Thanks for the encouragement," Joe chided.

"You're welcome," Li said and smiled over the rim of her cup.

"Anyway," Joe continued, "Li told me a little story about bamboo that I'll never forget."

Li examined Keith, and he squirmed inside like a first grader being scrutinized by the new headmaster. "What do you know about bamboo?" she queried.

"Well," Keith answered and began to grow warmer by the second, "uh…is this a pop quiz? Is there, like, going to be a grade?"

"Of course," Li said and never cracked a smile.

Joe's chuckles rumbled like thunder deep in his chest.

"Actually," Keith leaned forward, "my wife Jenny planted some in our backyard a few years ago, but the stuff has barely grown." He set his cup near Joe's, slipped out of his jacket, and draped it on the love seat's arm. "Oh, and pandas like to eat it." The last comment elicited a groan from Joe.

"Okay," Li sighed. "You failed. You get an F." She drew an imaginary "F" in the air.

Keith winced. "That's becoming a habit these days."

"Like most people, you know almost nothing about bamboo." Li enjoyed a long swallow of tea, then set the cup on the table with a dainty rattle. "Let's begin." She rubbed her hands together. "First of all, it is a grass and not a tree. There are more than 1200 varieties of bamboo, and it's grown on every continent except Antarctica. Some animals—pandas included—enjoy eating its leaves, but its best usage—aside from a great plant growing in your yard—is in what you can make from it."

She reached toward a nearby table, picked up a flat piece of wood, and handed it to Keith. He accepted the piece and was surprised at its weight…or lack of it.

"This is a cutting board made of bamboo," Li explained. "You could pound on this all day with a hammer and not dent it. Do you like it?"

"It's really nice. Do you sell these here?"

She smiled as she took the cutting board back from Keith. "Yes, we sell these. But I wouldn't dare part with this one. It was my grandmother's. It's been in my family for more than sixty years." She paused to watch Keith's expression. "Surprised, aren't you?"

"You might say that," he replied. "It looks brand-new!"

"Bamboo's a phenomenal plant. Strong as steel, and you can actually watch it grow—but only when it's ready." She stood and motioned toward the door. "You two cowboys get on your horse and come this way."

Keith eyed Joe. "Are you my horse?"

"Don't *even* think it!" Joe threatened.

"You guys are as bad as Charlie and Rick," Li teased and led the men from her office, through the store, and out to a small building in the nursery. She unlocked the door, pushed it open, walked in, and switched on the lights. Keith and Joe followed like good students. The first thing Keith noticed was the musty smell permeating the air—like old, used-up soil. He figured the empty, dirt-smeared containers on the shelves were the source of the odor. What space the containers didn't claim, gardening tools did—shovels, pruning shears, gloves.

"Forgive the mess," Li apologized. "This is not usually part of the tour, so I don't keep it as organized." She stood on her tiptoes, gripped the edge of a shelf, shoved aside this, and mumbled over that. "Ah, here it is," Li said as she grabbed a lengthy, rope-like object with bits of dirt dangling from long hairy fingers. On one end was a green-and-brown, cane-like shoot about a foot long.

"This was going to be a bamboo plant that would have stood at least fifteen feet tall by the end of the summer. But the customer who bought this from me two years ago got too impatient." Pointing to the foot-long cane, she said, "When he took it home this 'culm' was this tall." She then pointed to its root. "But its 'rhizome' was only a few inches long. He planted this in the corner of his yard where he wanted it to grow."

Keith crossed his arms, narrowed his eyes, and tried to play a mental game of connect the dots. *What does this have to do with soil preparation and wheat seeds?* he wondered.

Her features animated, Li continued. "The first year, nothing happened. Last year, nothing happened." She paused and pointed to the root. "Nothing *above ground*, that is. So he thought it was dead and dug it up." She wagged her head from side to side like a judge thoroughly disgusted with the latest criminal. "All nine feet of this rhizome!" Li lifted the root and dropped it. The thing swayed like a sluggish boa constrictor. "I told him when he bought it that it would take time to see growth, but he couldn't wait."

"If he had waited only *two more months*," she lifted two fingers, "he would have seen at least twelve canes come up from this rhizome. *Twelve!*" Her eyes widened behind thick glasses, and she looked like a bug-eyed grasshopper.

Keith leaned forward, then shot a glance at Joe. The guy appeared as mesmerized by the hairy root as Keith was beginning to feel.

"They would have grown to at least fifteen feet within a week or two—just this year alone. In the next several years, he would have had a bamboo colony made up of dozens of strong canes. But he couldn't wait. So he dug this up and asked for a new one. You know what? I gave him another one, and—"

"A piece of your mind with it?" Joe interrupted.

"Why would you evah think that?" Li laid her hand across her chest and fluttered her eyelashes.

Keith laughed out loud.

"Now the man has to wait another three years before he can enjoy bamboo in his yard!" Her lips twisting, Li threw the plant toward the back of the greenhouse shed and walked out.

Keith and Joe followed. Keith could think of nothing but the bamboo in his own backyard. He remembered the day Jenny planted it shortly after they bought the house. Between the two of them, she was the plant guru. Keith was just in charge of watering…or, rather, having the sprinkler system installed. On that warm, summer day Jenny had explained that the bamboo would look like it wasn't doing a thing for a few years. Then one day it would shoot up overnight. The growth had just begun during the last year. The root system must be every bit as great as the one Li had just shown him.

If only the roots went that deep in my marriage, Keith worried. For *him* they did. Keith just didn't know if Jenny would even come close to respecting him if she knew…

"Look, I have a gift for you!" Li said as they moseyed back into the gift shop. She stepped to the cash register, picked up two bamboo key rings, and handed one each to the men.

"Thanks," Joe said and rubbed the piece of bamboo like it was gold.

"Yeah, thanks." Keith stroked the slick cane, allowing his thumb to pause over each imperfection. *Oh God*, he prayed, *show me what You're trying to teach me…and what I need to do.*

Immediately his mind was filled with all that Joe had told him, including his admonishment to tell Jenny everything. Keith sighed. *Okay*, he continued, *I guess You've been showing me what to do for days now. Maybe it's just time for me to be a better listener.*

"What do ya say, Keith?" Joe asked.

Keith blinked and gazed from Joe to Li and back to Joe. "Excuse me?"

"Li was just asking us if we'd like her to show us around the big greenhouse." He pointed toward the large windows along the back of the gift shop.

"Oh sure!" Keith agreed and gazed toward a massive greenhouse that probably housed enough bamboo for a few thousand cutting boards. He noticed a large truck being filled with bamboo plants. Near the truck stood Charlie and Rick. It looked like Charlie was doing all the talking, and for once, Rick appeared fascinated and quite impressed. Ironically, he held a piece of brown bamboo that suspiciously resembled a fishing pole.

"You must ship all over the place," Keith said.

"Yep!" Li's smile couldn't have been more proud. "Charlie's helped me expand the business. I could have never done it without him." Her face glowed as her attention rested on her husband.

Keith looked down and wondered what Jenny was thinking right now…and if she'd ever look at him like that again.

Chapter Fourteen

"So what are you thinking?" Joe asked as the log cabin came into view, and he drove the truck into the driveway. Although the sun now blasted the countryside, small puddles filled the yard and the planted field appeared bathed and new.

Keith ceased from tormenting his bamboo keychain. He'd rubbed the thing like it was some kind of a magic genie bottle all the way from Li's Place. Keith had been driven deeper and deeper into thought from the moment he stepped into the massive greenhouse and was overwhelmed in the presence of so much bamboo. Everything Joe said and Li implied had come together in a message that he could no longer avoid or deny. If Keith was going to get out of the financial crater he was in, he'd have to make some lifestyle and thought pattern adjustments. He was convinced it wasn't going to happen any other way.

He looked at Joe, who put the truck into park. "I've been thinking about everything—what you said and what Li said too. I guess, in a nutshell, it all boils down to realizing that God uses hard times to till our 'soil,'" he drew invisible quotes in the air, "and we can choose to plant seed or not. If we plant the seed, then growth will happen. If we don't, then we've done nothing but stay exactly where we are—or maybe even stagnate." He gazed at the bamboo and rolled it against his palm. "And, like you said this morning and Li said about the bamboo, we can't always see the growth that's happening. Sometimes it takes a while, but in time you really do reap what you sow."

Joe turned off the engine and shifted to face Keith. His brows raised, he exclaimed, "You got it!"

"Yeah…and why do you have to look so surprised about it? Maybe I'm not as hardheaded as you thought, huh?"

Joe rubbed the corners of his mouth and looked away. "Maybe not," he finally said and chuckled. He eagerly leaned forward. "Remember, it doesn't matter how small the seed is. It just needs a chance to grow. What I've been trying to say all this time is if all you do is make money and spend it just as fast, it would be the same as if we harvested the wheat and ground it all into flour. Sure, we would have enough flour for all of our baking for a while, but come next year what would I use to start the next crop? If you spend all your money on you—even if it *is* for necessary stuff—you won't have any seed left for the next crop."

"Yeah, I already thought about that," Keith admitted and sighed.

"Well, guess what?" Joe removed the keys from the ignition, and jangled them against his palm. "It's the same with your time and talents. Give and it shall be given unto you! I have lived this!" Joe lifted his hands like a Sunday-morning preacher.

Keith mimicked him. "Are you going to be announcing the choir soon?" he teased.

"I might." Joe relaxed against the seat and rested his head upon the headrest. "Whew! This has been a tough three days. You've worn me out."

Noticing the dark shadows under Joe's eyes, Keith hesitated to voice his next observation. The truck was getting stuffy anyway, and his jacket was feeling heavier by the minute. *Maybe it's better to take this conversation inside*, he thought, then eyed Marcy's Chevy. He decided to go ahead. Once inside, they'd have all sorts of distractions. He might as well finish this now so Joe could rest later.

"Would you say the Cycle of Giving is like investing?"

Joe's lids slid open, and he eyed Keith with a sideways stare.

"Nope," he said and lifted his head. "Well…" he looked toward the woods, "maybe. Except usually you put your money in a safe place where you're guaranteed a return."

"Well, some of us have been known to take chances." Keith slipped his keychain into his pocket.

"Humph, yep," Joe agreed. "I'm not saying it's *bad* to have investments. Marcy and I do have a habit of saving. But if that's all you're doing, you still haven't even touched what I've been saying." He opened his door, and Keith followed suit. A cooling draft swept across the men like a river of air. "The best place to sow your seed," Joe continued, "is where there won't be a noticeable harvest—like giving to those who maybe can't repay you or have no intentions of ever repaying you."

"Why does that not surprise me?" Keith mumbled and pinched his lower lip. "I guess you've got suggestions on that too."

"How'd you guess?" Joe asked.

"Just lucky, I guess." Keith wiped a streak of dust from the front of his jeans. "So shoot!" He leveled a direct stare across the truck cab to his friend.

"Church." Joe never blinked. "Those people *never* pay back contributions."

Keith chuckled. "You got that one right." He sat back, crossed his arms, and narrowed his eyes. "Jenny and I used to do church," he mused. Gazing upward, he tried to remember when they'd stopped attending and why. The answer eluded him. In his memory, there was no line of demarcation, just a gradual waning that eventually led to no attendance at all.

"We used to be really active, actually," he added. "The first year we were married, we were there every Sunday and then some. I helped with the newsletter and outreach. Jenny was in the middle of the seniors ministry. We even…"

Keith paused and recalled his farming grandma putting an envelope in the offering plate. Even though his parents hadn't been big churchgoers, his grandparents had been some of the most faithful members and givers. His praying grandma always said, "Givin' to church is the same as givin' to God. They do the Lord's business and that makes a giver part of that business."

His grandparents were a large part of the reason Keith went to church as an adult. His grandmother would call every Saturday, reminding him the next day was Sunday. Keith had started attending in college just so he wouldn't have to tell his grandmother he hadn't gone. One thing led to another until he was as faithful a giver as his grandparents were. Now, they'd both passed on, and Keith's parents were too busy to even think about church—let alone encourage their son to attend. But that's the way it always had been with them. Looking back, Keith realized he'd learned more from his grandparents than from his parents, and he'd already vowed never to make that mistake with his own children.

If I ever have any children, he thought bitterly. *I might not have a wife by the time this is all over.*

"You even…" Joe prompted.

Keith blinked and shifted his attention back to Joe. "Oh! I didn't finish, did I?"

"Not quite."

"I was just saying we even gave money…uh…regularly."

"Maybe God allowed all this to happen to jolt you back to where you started," Joe commented with a sage nod.

"Maybe so," Keith agreed and eyed the freshly planted field. "Maybe so."

Joe pointed toward the field. "You know what stalks I use for the seed I save for the next year?"

"Which ones?"

He pushed the truck door wide open. "The best ones," he said. "Not the leftovers—the top of the pile. I give God my best too. Think about it. The best wheat seed is going to produce the best crop. Same holds true with talent, money, priorities, and God. You really can't outgive Him." Joe slid out of the truck and faced his friend. "Like I've already said, you won't get a harvest if you don't plant seed. And it doesn't matter how small the seed is at the start. As your harvest increases, you'll be able to plant more and more. I personally guarantee it, Keith. It's worked for Marcy and me." He motioned toward the field they planted yesterday. It was an expansion project, and this was the first year they'd planted that plot. "It'll work for you and Jenny too." He closed his door, walked toward the front of the truck, and bent to pet Spot.

Keith got out and welcomed the cool breeze. He slammed his door, approached the dog, and offered an ear scratch or two that was repaid with a round of wet licks.

"There is a company based in Montana called Great Harvest

Bread," Joe said. "Part of their mission statement is to give generously. They've found that the more bread they give away, the more they sell. The same is true in our lives. We give a good bit of our grain to a co-op that, in turn, grinds it into flour and gives it to needy families in the Seattle area. It seems the more we give to the co-op, the bigger our next harvest is. It really is that simple."

"I think you've finally made a believer out of me," Keith said and fingered the bamboo keychain in his pocket. He thought about the hundred dollar bill in his billfold and decided to put Joe's wisdom into practice as soon as he could. *The first chance I got to plant part of that baby, I'm all over it.*

"The only thing I've got left to say," Joe added, "is that there's a balance to everything. I'm not saying you take every paycheck and put the whole thing in the offering plate while you've got bills to pay. I believe God expects us to take care of our obligations and our families just as much as He wants us to give to others."

"I understand," Keith agreed. "But I guess I've just been too selfish lately to even give a dime. I've been more interested in building my own empire." He winced and hated the taste of confession, but he understood that confession was a must before regeneration could begin.

"And another thing," Joe continued, "I don't think it's a good idea to give to people you know are going to take the money and use it for drugs and such. That's the same as handing them a bag of marijuana or cocaine or whatever it is they're on."

"Right."

Joe began strolling toward the front door, and Keith fell in beside him. "When I first met Li," Joe said, "I was on the verge of shutting the coffee shop. I had just about used up all of our savings." He paused and stared toward the horizon, as if he were watching a replay of a tragic movie. "Marcy and I were beginning to question why I had given up my job. The stress was really getting to both of us. We weren't exactly acting like honeymooners either…" he lifted his brows, "…if you get my drift."

"Got it," Keith acknowledged and didn't add that he was living the same misery.

Joe stepped toward the house again. "And even though we had planted lots of seed—to church and missions and even a local homeless rescue—you know how much growth we were seeing?" Joe lifted his hand and formed a zero with his thumb and index finger. "Nada."

"Sounds like my luck these days." Keith walked up the steps.

"I was about to close Mac's Place." Joe's boots scuffed against the porch. "And ask for my old job back when Li came in." He lifted his hands. "Changed everything. I remember her looking at me through those glasses of hers and asking, 'How do you know tomorrow isn't the day you'll see growth?'" Joe leaned forward and mimicked Li's glare. "'How do you know next week won't be harvest time?'" He paused with his hand on the doorknob. "Then she dragged me out to that bamboo place of hers and preached me a sermon."

Keith's laugh winged across the porch. Spot woofed a protest.

"And you know what?" Joe bent to pat Spot. "She was right, almost to the day. By the end of the next week my ex-boss at the ad agency came into Mac's Place. He ordered a large latte, even though he had no idea what a latte was. Then he asked if he could pay with a check. He pulled out an envelope and handed it to me. Inside was a check big enough to cover my salary and expenses for the next six months."

"Good grief!" Keith rocked back on his heels.

"Exactly." His eyes widening, Joe nodded. "He said a client I had designed a campaign for had insisted I participate in the earnings from that campaign—even though I was no longer with the agency. And to think I almost quit before the harvest came."

Joe turned the doorknob, and Keith could only hope something similar might happen to him. He followed his friend into the cozy home that smelled of homemade bread and lacked the high-fashion polish of his house in Detroit. But amid the crocheted throws and rock fireplace and worn ottoman, something else was present that Keith longed for. Something unseen and intangible. Something called peace.

Right now Keith would give his right arm to know that his and Jenny's life could be straightened out, and they could start over. Maybe if they were given the chance, they could stick to the plan and do things right.

Joe shut the door and rubbed his hands together. "Smells like Marcy's cooking." Looking like a hungry schoolboy, Joe shed his jacket. Keith was right behind him.

With their jackets swinging from the hooks near the door, the two men hurried toward the source of the smells. But as he neared the kitchen, Keith realized Marcy was talking to someone… another female who sounded familiar. As Joe traipsed into the kitchen, Keith stopped on the threshold and couldn't force himself to move another inch. A petite, blonde woman stood near Marcy at the oven. The two of them were bending over, looking into the oven, and chattering like two campers at a bonfire.

When she straightened, Marcy held a pan of freshly baked bread. She caught sight of Joe and greeted him with a quick peck.

"Looks like you're up to your old habits, huh?" Joe hovered over a cooling rack that held two brown loaves that looked too perfect to be real. Never once did he act as if he were surprised to see the blonde.

Keith's palms flashed hot—like a teenager about to pick up his first date. Except she was the homecoming queen, and he was the class nerd. His head spun with a barrage of mystified questions that found no answers and only spawned more confusion. The blonde turned off the oven, swiveled from Joe and Marcy, and threw a cautious glance toward the doorway. As his wife's gaze met his, Keith received the distinct impression that *he* was the only one surprised by this turn of events.

"Jenny?" And for a zany second he wondered if he were seeing an apparition…or a hallucination.

"Hi, Keith," she said, and her tremulous voice assured Keith that Jenny was here in the flesh.

Chapter Fifteen

"Jenny!" Keith repeated, his voice squeaking.

Joe crossed his arms, leaned against a cabinet, and smiled at his friend. Marcy hung on to Joe's arm and shouted, "Surprise!"

"But how…" Keith gaped awhile, then closed his mouth and swallowed against the lump in his throat.

"We had some frequent flier miles," Marcy explained, "and thought we'd just…" She shrugged and gazed up at her husband. The two looked at each other like they'd pulled off the scheme of the century. Keith was stricken with how well they complemented each other—right down to their worn blue jeans. Marcy was far from a slender, beauty-queen type, but she offered an ease of spirit and comfort of soul that transcended words.

Keith cast his attention back to his wife and remembered the days when he'd thought the two of them complemented each other just as well. Jenny, forever meticulously groomed, was pretty as always, and Keith recalled the first time they met in the singles' group at church.

"Well…I, uh…" Joe cleared his throat, "guess we'll mosey on outta here."

"Yeah," Marcy chimed in, "I think we have some carrots to peel in the laundry room, or…or dog treats to count, or, um," she lamely waved her hand, "or something."

As they passed, Joe punched Keith in the arm. He leaned close and whispered, "Break a leg."

"I'm going to break *your* leg for not telling me," Keith growled back.

Joe snickered as he and Marcy disappeared.

Jenny's stiff smile faltered. She clung to the counter.

"So, um, hi," Keith said and eyed the kitchen table, the checked curtains, the refrigerator, his work boots, and then the top of Jenny's head.

"You're not mad, are you? I mean—that I came like this?" Jenny questioned.

"No!" Keith exclaimed.

She jumped.

"Oh!" He stepped forward and halted. "I didn't—didn't mean to scare you."

"It's okay." She raised both hands, palms outward. And Keith noticed her hands were trembling as badly as his legs. Furthermore, the helplessness in her big, brown eyes did little to ease his nerves.

Keith knew the time had come. He *had* to tell her. No more stalling. No more trying to find a way to get out of it. Jenny needed to know. And if Keith was any kind of a man, he would come clean.

"Want to go sit on the porch swing?" he asked, his voice ringing with hollow resignation.

"Sure." Jenny swallowed and gradually grew pale.

She looks like she's going to her own funeral, Keith thought. When she walked past him, he noticed she was wearing his favorite pantsuit—a slinky, yellow number that brought out the sparkle in her eyes. He also recognized the faint scent of wildflowers. He'd gotten her the whole set of bath stuff last Christmas. That now seemed like years ago.

As Jenny neared the door, he forced his feet to move and wondered if perhaps this was *his* funeral, not Jenny's. *Or maybe, it's our marriage's funeral,* he thought and nearly drowned in a wave of nausea. He loved Jenny more than ever. These three days of separation had done nothing but magnify his need for the woman he'd vowed to honor and cherish.

By the time they'd slipped on their jackets and Jenny settled onto the swing, Keith was tempted to fall at her feet and beg her forgiveness before ever breaking the news. He was desperate enough to do nearly anything at this point. Nothing seemed too ridiculous.

Her head bent, Jenny watched Keith from the corner of her eyes. The swing rocked and squeaked as he sat next to her. The man was as stiff as a corpse. Jenny's mind raced with a myriad of wild possibilities. While the other woman scenario wasn't completely out of the picture, she'd imagined all sorts of other things during the night—like drug addiction…a deadly illness…a 30-something midlife crisis…or even gender issues.

Her eyes stinging, Jenny wished Keith would just come out with it. Marcy certainly wouldn't leak a syllable. She'd simply called yesterday and asked Jenny if she'd like a free trip to Washington. Jenny had grabbed the chance. She'd thrown a few things into a bag, put Boots in a cattery, and jumped onto the plane before she ever questioned her decision.

But now Keith seemed farther away than ever. He stared toward the freshly tilled field like the dirt somehow held answers. To what, Jenny didn't know. But she knew she had to find out. She simply couldn't take another second of this torture.

When he leaned forward, placed his elbows on his knees, and cradled his head in his hands, Jenny dared touch his arm. "Keith," she said, "whatever it is, please tell me. I can't take this anymore."

He stiffened, then mumbled something against his hands that sounded like he was saying he lost something.

Wrinkling her brow, Jenny leaned closer. "What?" she asked and strained for his meaning.

Standing, Keith strode to the porch rail and gripped it until his knuckles whitened.

Wishing she could will him to speak, Jenny mutely stared at her husband's back. He looked leaner in the jeans and work shirt than in his business suits. Or maybe he *was* leaner.

If he's got a terrible illness, then it must be making him lose weight! Jenny's pulse grew wild and erratic and panic snatched her breath.

Finally Keith blurted, "I lost your inheritance. And we're on the verge of bankruptcy."

Jenny's fingers curled around the swing's armrest. "What?" she squeaked as a wave of dismay rocked her world.

Keith swiveled toward her, his face pale, haunted. "We're broke," he said, his lips stiff. "I made a wrong move—or a *few* wrong moves—in the stock market and lost your inheritance." He doubled his fists and swayed. "My bonuses haven't been as high this year as I thought they would be. That, plus losing the interest income from your money, has cut our income way down. I haven't been able to pay off our credit card bills because of the car and house payments. We're up to our eyeballs in credit card debt right now. And I'm the biggest fraud of the century. I'm a financial advisor!" He pressed his fingers against his chest. "I'm supposed to be good with money."

Her numb mind jumped to the day she rescued Boots and her credit cards kept being declined. "So that explains why the cards were refused at PetSmart," she muttered as the dismay escalated to shock.

"PetSmart?" Keith asked. "What were you doing there?"

"Buying stuff for Boots," Jenny answered and stared up at him without even a blink. In a detached sort of way she knew she was saying too much, but her mind was too numb to stop the flow.

"Who's Boots?"

"My cat," she explained as the reality of what Keith had just admitted seeped into her soul. "I adopted him the other day when I—" Jenny finally found the will to stop herself. She ducked her head and clamped her teeth on her bottom lip. She'd come within a breath of telling Keith she was the firm's prowler.

Broke. We're broke? How can that be?

Jenny had *never* been broke. Growing up, she'd lived in the ritzy part of town and had been one of the better-off kids at school. Her father was one of the most respected and renowned cancer specialists on the West coast. His expertise had rewarded him soundly. When Jenny married Keith, her new husband had already made enough through investments to live on for a year should the need arise. When they moved to Detroit and bought their house, they sank the majority of that money into the equity. Then Jenny's mother died and left what Jenny thought would be her nest egg for life. Ironically, Keith's abilities with money had made Jenny feel as secure as when she was growing up. In all her bizarre brainstorms, she'd never even considered the problem could be financial.

This is bad, she thought, *but not half as bad as anything I've imagined. At least it doesn't involve death or another woman.*

A thin trickle of relief mingled with the onslaught of financial stress. Her death grip on the swing arm eased. Jenny crossed her arms and hugged herself as an unexpected whimper escaped her. She imagined herself wearing hair curlers and a stained dress, driving up to a garage sale in a rusty, 1960 Plymouth. Her emotions rocked from one extreme to another, and a hysterical giggle followed the whimper.

Now it was her turn to cover her face. The giggle opened up the gate to full-blown hilarity. She'd been so worried that Keith's problem involved a lover, drug abuse, or death that she'd prepared herself for the worst. And while the money loss wasn't exactly what she'd have chosen, it was nothing compared to the other scenarios.

"Jenny?" The swing jiggled with Keith's weight. "Did you understand me?" he snapped. "We're broke!"

Her laughter escalating, Jenny pictured herself sneaking into the firm, spilling tea all over Mr. Rothingham, then facing him in her front yard when she was looking for Boots. It was all just too crazy!

Jenny doubled forward and clutched her midsection. "Is that all?" she wheezed. "There's no more news?"

"Well, yeah, that's all, and no, there's no more news."

"You mean there's really not another woman...or—or man?"

"What?" he yelled and stood. The swing lunged into a wild zigzag.

Leaning back, Jenny mopped at her eyes and looked up at her husband, who glared at her like she'd gone nuts. Maybe she had. This whole thing had nearly eaten her up—to the point where she'd been willing to break the law. A final round of giggles teetered out.

"What about Celia then?" she blurted before she even thought.

"Celia?" he croaked.

"I found that Christmas picture of her sitting in your lap. She had on a Santa hat, and—" Jenny's damp eyes widened. "Oh no!" she yelped. "I can't believe I said that!"

"Where'd you find *that* picture?" Keith demanded.

Jenny's only answer was a bug-eyed stare while a slow tremor attacked her every nerve.

"I tried to get her to give that picture to me when her secretary took it, but they wouldn't!" Keith's face reddened. "She jumped in my lap at the Christmas party, and then the flash happened before I even knew what hit me. You've got to believe me, Jenny!" he bellowed. "I had to nearly beat her off before she went in for a kiss. You've got to believe me!" Keith repeated and raised his hands.

"I...I..."

"Where did you find the picture, anyway?" He placed his hands on his hips.

"I believe you," Jenny rushed, and she really meant it.

Keith blinked and stared into her soul. Finally he dropped next to Jenny, gripped her hands, and his dark eyes held a tortured appeal that wrenched her soul.

"There's no other woman, and there never has been. And I want more than your just saying you believe me this time. I want to know if you're *ever* going to trust me *for good*," he demanded, his gaze growing intense. "When you accuse me, it makes me feel like—like *dirt*, and I haven't even done anything wrong. I've never given you one reason not to trust me. Not one!"

As the plea hung between them, a veil of defeat snuffed out the exasperation, and Keith lowered his gaze. "At least not with our marriage," he corrected.

His words pierced Jenny's heart with regret and pain. "You're right," she agreed. "I've been a jealous maniac, and it's made me do and think all sorts of things that are all wrong. I guess it's because—because I'm afraid somehow...I—I—" Jenny shook her head and swallowed hard. "I don't think I've ever gotten over feeling like my birth mother rejected me. Then my adoptive parents both died so young. I think I've been terrified that you'd eventually be taken away too."

"Jenny, you mean more to me than anything!" Keith's fingers tightened around hers.

She pulled her hand from his and stroked his face. His skin felt as smooth as always, with but a faint prick of whiskers. "I feel the same way," she whispered.

He covered her hand with his and pressed his lips inside her palm. "I've been thinking." He dubiously eyed her and lowered their hands. "If we sold the house, we could recoup the equity and pay off everything...maybe even trade in the Mercedes and Porsche for economy cars. We'd be completely out of debt and maybe still have enough to put down on a small townhouse."

Images of her beloved house floated into Jenny's mind. She'd put her heart and soul into that place. The problem was, she'd also spent like a monster to get it where it was. But Keith never told her not to. "Why didn't you *tell* me before I spent so much?" Jenny asked.

Keith looked away. "Because I kept thinking I'd recover, and you'd never have to know. Do you know what it does to a man to have to tell his wife he's been such a failure?"

Jenny gripped his hands. "Oh, Keith, I...you should have told me. You should have *trusted* me enough to know I'd—"

"Can you ever forgive me?" His head drooped like a boy who's been caught stealing.

She nodded and knew the forgiveness had already happened. "Yes...but I'll be honest, I *do* have some questions, and I know not having money is going to be hard to get—to get used to." She eyed her diamond-studded Rolex. "And if I have to give up the house, I just do. Really, compared to our marriage and all the insane things I was worried about, well," she shrugged, "there's just no comparison. In a lot of ways I'm relieved this is all it is. Last night I even started worrying that maybe you were dying from some disease."

A cool droplet dripped onto her fingers, and Jenny realized her husband's lowered eyes were producing the moisture. Her eyes stung anew.

"I think that's why I started laughing," she admitted and laid her hand on his shoulder. "I was so relieved that's *all* it was."

"But I really feel like I've betrayed you," Keith mourned and slumped against the back of the swing.

Jenny lowered her head and grappled with what to say next. Finally she was overcome with the conviction of what that should be. It hurt to admit, but the truth sometimes did bring pain.

"And I've...be–betrayed you." Jenny lifted her gaze to his. "I've accused you of things you've never even thought of doing."

With a deep sigh, Keith scrubbed at the tears with the back of his free hand.

"Also…" Jenny added, and she debated whether or not to tell all. Finally she decided that Keith had been honest with her, and she should be just as honest with him. She cleared her throat. "You asked me where I found the photo of you and Celia…"

Keith turned his attention to her and waited, his expression laced with curiosity.

"Well, uh…" Jenny looked down, "I, uh, sorta…" Her pulse pounding, she took a deep breath and plunged forward. "I was the one who broke into the firm."

"You!" His eyes wide, Keith sat straight up. His mouth hung open. He looked at Jenny like she'd just told him she robbed a bank.

"Yes, me," she admitted. She told him the whole story, confessing her motivation as well.

Groaning, he covered his face before gruffly rubbing it. "You could have been arrested!"

"I know," she said in a tiny voice that sounded like it belonged to a mouse. She pressed at the faint crease along the front of her pants.

Keith slumped forward. "If Mr. Rothingham ever finds out, I'm out of a job!"

"He won't!" she insisted and gripped his upper arm. "Why should he? He has no clue. He looked right at me the other day and never acted like he connected me with the prowler at all."

"Are you sure?" He turned doubtful eyes to her.

"Absolutely!" Jenny nodded. "I nearly laughed in his face when he was telling me about the break-in—when he was warning me to be careful."

"Why does that not surprise me?" Keith groaned.

Jenny shifted away from him and added, "Anyway, that's where

I got Boots. He was in the alley behind the offices, and I felt sorry for him." She picked at a hangnail and couldn't remember a time when her nails had ever looked so bad or she had ever cared less.

Keith rested his knees on his elbows and locked his fingers. Jenny noticed his shoulders shaking only seconds before a rumble of deep laughter tumbled out. Mere minutes away from her own fit with hilarity, Jenny couldn't stop a few nervous giggles.

"We're a fine pair, aren't we?" he said through his chuckles. "A bankrupt financial planner and his criminal wife!"

Chapter Sixteen

An hour later, Keith and Jenny still sat in the swing. With his arm around Jenny, Keith enjoyed the feel of her head on his shoulder. Many months had passed since they'd sat and talked like they had this afternoon. Keith told her everything Joe shared about planting and harvesting. He promised her he'd gain back her inheritance if it took him the rest of his life.

"You know," Jenny said as she shifted and slipped her arm around Keith's midsection, "maybe God allowed all this to happen so we would go back to where we started. Really, I never even realized how far we'd drifted until the last few days. I guess I'd gotten too independent and, well, sassy. I mean, what did I need God for? What did we need to give for? We had everything!"

Keith stroked Jenny's arm. "Yes, I thought something very similar last night. But really, I'm realizing that even if you're the richest person in the world, if you don't have the Lord and a good relationship at home, then you really have nothing."

Jenny lifted her head. With her face inches from his, Keith was hard-pressed to concentrate on what she was saying…something about her agreeing…which was a good thing because he was ready to put the kiss of approval on their new start. Just as he was leaning in for the treasure and Jenny's eyes were fluttering shut, the front door opened.

Both jerked back like two teens caught by a parent.

Joe eased out the door and sheepishly eyed the couple. "Sorry," he said, "but Marcy's sending me to town." He rattled his keys and pointed toward his truck in the driveway. "I'll just, uh, be on my way."

He was halfway down the steps before Keith untangled himself from Jenny and stood. "Wait!" he called. "There's something I want you to do." Keith hurried toward his friend, who pivoted on the steps and squinted against the afternoon sunshine. Pulling out his billfold, Keith grabbed Rick's $100 bill and shoved it toward Joe. "Take this and go to the seafood deli. Buy as much lobster as you think you can hold. Oh, and an extra-large shrimp ring too. Marcy loves those, right?"

Joe held up both hands. "I can't take that," he protested, "it's just about all the money you have right now."

Keith cocked his head and stared Joe down. "Are you the same guy who's been talking to me about sowing the last few days?"

"Yeah, but Keith, seafood is *high!* I could spend *half* this easy!"

"When I said I couldn't take the money from Rick, you said I *had* to or I'd mess up the whole cycle. Remember? You and Marcy just sowed your frequent flier miles to buy Jenny a plane ticket. Now, this is *your* harvest and my way of planting too."

"Looks like my words are coming back to haunt me."

"So if the seafood costs half this, then I'm planting half," Keith asserted. "Now, let's see what happens."

Joe took the money and shook his head. "I guess you listened closer than I thought," he said.

"Besides," Keith added, "Jenny and I decided to sell the house and use the equity to get out of debt. We're not on skid row yet."

"Okay," Joe said and nodded. "Sounds like a plan."

"Let's plant it *all*, Keith!" Scurrying to his side, Jenny stepped into the circle of his arm and gave a joyous hug. "Buy one of those gourmet cheesecakes too, Joe, and a bunch of flowers, and…and… rent a movie or something! Use it all on tonight. It will be our gift to you—a celebration!"

"But—" Joe started.

Spot's barking preceded his appearance from around the house.

"See, Spot even agrees!" Keith exclaimed.

Joe laughed. "All right! All right!" he raised his hands. "I'm willing soil. I won't spit the seed back at you." He bent to pet the German shepherd as he stopped near his owner. "What's your favorite movie, Jenny?" Joe asked.

"Uuuuhhhh…" Jenny looked at Keith.

"How 'bout *It's a Wonderful Life?*" Joe prompted.

"Great!" Jenny exclaimed. "I haven't seen that one in ages, and I love it."

"Good." Joe's sage nod and knowing smile hinted at a hidden message, and Keith strained for his friend's motive.

But as his wife stirred against him, he decided to figure it out later. Before Joe reached the truck, Keith pulled Jenny closer and stole a quick kiss that promised more to come. Pulling away, he stroked Jenny's cheek, peered into her eyes that were full of adoration, and couldn't remember a time he'd ever felt so free.

"Listen, Daddy. Teacher says every time a bell rings, an angel gets its wings."

"That's right, that's right," said Jimmy Stewart's character, George Bailey. "Atta boy, Clarence."

As the credits rolled at the end of *It's A Wonderful Life*, Joe stood and switched on the lights. The fireplace's smoldering coals blurred as Jenny discreetly dabbed at her damp eyes. Then she noticed Marcy was wiping a tear from her cheek. The two caught each other's eyes, and Marcy soundly sniffed.

Jenny giggled and fished in her pocket for another tissue. "This movie gets me every time."

"Me too," Marcy said. "I always cry when the people bring in all of their money to help George. Even though I've watched it scores of times, I still cry."

"So," Keith leaned toward the coffee table and looked toward Joe, "do we guess why you thought this movie was so appropriate or are you just going to come out and tell us?" He dug into the half-full bowl of popcorn and tossed a few kernels into his mouth.

Groaning, Jenny clutched her midsection. "How can you *eat* any more after all that seafood?" she questioned. Jenny reached for her glass of water and sipped the tart liquid that was laced with lemon slices. Even though the ice had melted long ago, the water was by far preferable to buttery popcorn. Joe had taken them at their word and bought a feast fit for a whole ship's crew. Jenny didn't think she'd *ever* be hungry again. "I'm still full, and I didn't eat any popcorn in the first place."

Keith smiled at Jenny. "I'm a growin' boy," he teased, and Jenny recalled the early days of their relationship when she'd been so charmed by his dimples and that carefree light in his eyes. Now she didn't care if they never had another dime. The peace that had settled upon their relationship was worth *two* inheritances.

As their gaze lengthened, Joe's voice boomed upon the moment, "Okay, you two! There are people here, ya know!"

Jenny ducked her head, and Keith twined his fingers with hers. "So…that was George's harvest, right?" he asked, his voice thick with humor. "All that money people gave him at the end?"

"Ah! You figured it out!" Joe said.

"I'm not half as thick-skulled as I look," Keith said.

"And it's a good thing," Joe teased.

Keith shot him a feigned glare while Joe reached for the popcorn and settled the whole bowl in his lap. After several bites, he said, "Actually, there was sowing and reaping in the whole movie. That's why I suggested this one. It's a classic example." He pointed toward the screen where credits now scrolled.

Marcy stood, stretched, picked up the remote, and turned off the television. "I'll get everyone more drinks," she offered and reached for Jenny's tired water. "I feel a movie critique coming on." She winked at her husband. "We could be here awhile."

"Go ahead. Mock me, why don't you?" Joe set aside the bowl and huffed.

"Oh, poor baby," Marcy teased and moved to her husband's side. "Did I hurt your feewings?" She bent to kiss his forehead before picking up his empty glass. Then she said, "Would you prefer I call you Ebert or Roeper?"

Joe rolled his eyes. "Oh brother," he said and snatched the glass. "Give me my glass. I know when I'm not appreciated. I'll just get my own drink, thank you very much."

Snickering, Marcy swiftly exited with Joe close behind. A faint squeal erupted the second they left the room.

"I guess we'll have to figure out the rest ourselves," Keith said.

Jenny eyed the time-worn grandfather clock claiming the corner. Even though the chimes vibrated with eight dongs, it was eleven in Detroit. A wide yawn overtook her.

"Let's escape while we can," Keith whispered.

Jenny gazed from the homey living room toward the kitchen. "But wouldn't that be, like, rude?"

After a high-pitched giggle tottered from the kitchen, Keith smirked. "I seriously doubt they'll even notice."

As much as Jenny wanted to answer the invitation in Keith's eyes, she hated acting like an ungrateful guest. Just going to bed without telling their friends seemed like the fiercest of social sins.

"Why don't we at least tell them before Marcy gets our drinks," she compromised.

"Okay." He leaned closer and rested his forehead on Jenny's.

When his lips brushed hers, she found it tempting to forgo telling Joe and Marcy they were going to bed. But social graces won out.

By the time the two reached the top of the stairs and entered the loft room, Jenny felt like a teenager running away from home. But as the door closed on their union, she knew the two of them were coming back home…and starting over.

The next morning, Keith stirred in the narrow bed and realized there was someone with him. His eyes still closed, he recalled the previous evening and smiled while opening his eyes. A blonde-haired angel was propped on her elbow, watching him. She returned his smile and traced his lips with her fingertip.

"Hi," she said, her voice husky.

"Hi." Keith kissed the tip of her finger. "Am I dreaming or are you real?"

"Real," she affirmed without a blink.

"I can't believe you're here," he said before a languid yawn won out.

"Me neither," she replied and snuggled in closer.

"Hmmm," Keith said and loved the smell of her hair.

A faint whispering tugged Keith's attention to the door. A flash of white slashed the shadows near the floor and drew his gaze downward. An envelope lay on the wooden floor. "Looks like the mail has run," he said and glanced toward the clock on the night stand. His eyes bugged. "Oh my word! It's already nine o'clock!"

"Yep," Jenny said. "We slept late—*really* late."

"We're turning into slugs," Keith groaned. He tossed off the covers and knew that they'd both needed the rest. Jenny hadn't complained a bit, but jet lag usually knocked her out.

After a yawn, she flopped back on the pillow and stared at the ceiling. "Are you going to get the mail or do you want me to?" she asked.

"I'll get it," Keith said and quirked an eyebrow. "I wouldn't want you to exert yourself or anything."

She cut him a droll stare. "Watch it, buddy. I deliver a mean right."

Chuckling, Keith padded toward the envelope that had "Keith and Jenny" scrawled across the front in Joe's bold script. "Wonder who this is from?" he sarcastically quipped and tossed the envelope toward his wife. "You open it. Nature's calling."

As Keith went into the restroom, Jenny propped herself up on the pillows, opened the envelope, and withdrew a typed note.

Upon returning, Keith dropped onto the bed. He scooted close to Jenny and said, "What's he saying?"

"I've barely skimmed it," Jenny explained and lifted the page. "Want to read it together?"

"You read it," Keith said. "I want to hear your voice."

Jenny couldn't stop the flirtatious smile. Feeling like a new-lywed, she cleared her throat. "I've got to make sure my voice sounds right," she added and dashed him a saucy glance before reading the note.

Keith and Jenny,

Really enjoyed our time last night. Thanks again for the dinner. Marcy and I will be out for the rest of the day. Feel free to enjoy the place. We left breakfast in the oven, but if you don't get up in time to eat, just give it to Spot. We also left the movie in the DVD player in case you want a rerun. Or rather, might I suggest a rerun. Next time, watch it with a pen and paper and take notes on how many times the sowing/reaping process shows up.

"You know..." Keith interrupted.

Jenny lowered the letter and eyed her husband, who was staring at the ceiling with his hand under his head.

"I've watched that movie a dozen times, and I've never given much thought to the sowing and reaping until last night."

"Me neither," Jenny admitted. "But maybe that's the reason we like it so much. Maybe we picked up on some of the subliminal meaning without realizing it."

Keith propped himself up on his elbow. "I'm all over it now," he rushed. "George sowed seed all during the movie. But then there's the $8,000 he got at the end from the townspeople. What seed did he plant then?"

Jenny pointed at her husband. "I know!" she exclaimed. "It was when he jumped off the bridge and saved Clarence's life."

Keith nodded and pointed back. "Right! He saved Clarence's life, and the townspeople saved his hide!" Keith stared across the room as if he'd merged into another universe.

"You've zoned out on me," Jenny commented.

"I'm thinking about bamboo," Keith asserted.

"Oh," Jenny said, her lips remaining puckered.

"Deep roots." He said and lifted his hand for emphasis. "You know more about it than I do. It takes a long time before you see growth, but its root system doesn't stop."

"Soooo..." Jenny encouraged.

"George," Keith said. "His roots went deep. When the pressure was on, his harvest came in anyway."

Jenny nodded, then gazed out the window toward a brilliant, blue sky. "I wonder how deep our roots are right now?" she asked.

"However far a hundred bucks will stretch," Keith finally said. "That's about all we've given in ages."

She stroked at the handmade quilt that served as their comforter. "We've got to do better from now on," she asserted.

Keith wrapped his hand around hers. "We will," he said. "I promise. We will."

Jenny looked into his eyes.

"After talking to Joe so much, I feel like we've really blown it in more ways than I ever imagined. Or at least *I've* blown it." He pressed his finger against his chest.

"We've *both* blown it," Jenny insisted and eyed the note before picking it back up.

"We never finished that, did we?" Keith asked.

In answer, Jenny started reading,

> *You two have impressed Marcy and me more than you can ever know. Last night you sowed every bit of extra money you had. Even though you did participate in the meal, we are convinced your motives were all for us and that God is pleased with your sacrifice and your effort. He will honor what you have done. Remember, be prepared for the harvest.*
>
> *Keith, thank you so much for coming to me with your situation. You showed me great honor by sharing your concerns with me. Now I want to ask you to show me one more honor by receiving a seed.*

"A seed?" Keith questioned.

"That's what it says." As the two examined the note, Jenny turned it over. She didn't spot anything to do with a seed.

Keith picked up the envelope, looked inside, and turned it sideways. A clear disk the size of a quarter whispered out and plopped onto his palm. He lifted the disk, and Jenny leaned closer to scrutinize the tiny speck in the center. It looked like a fleck of reddish-orange paint floating in the middle. It could be a seed—a very small one, but a seed nonetheless.

"That's cool," Jenny said and took the seed from Keith.

"Really," Keith mumbled.

Rubbing the smooth disk between forefinger and thumb, she continued to read,

> *Marcy and I wanted you and Jenny to have this tiny mustard seed. It might seem insignificant, but it's really a very*

powerful engine. There is a story that a mustard seed found its way into a batch of concrete being used for a building. The seed somehow sprouted in that concrete and forced its way through the building's foundation until it found sunlight. In doing so, it damaged the foundation so much that the building was condemned and had to be torn down. Do not take a tiny seed for granted. No matter how small the seed is you have to plant, plant it anyway and expect a great harvest.

Remember, when we give, God repays. You really can't outgive God! I know I've heard this somewhere lately....

All the best,
Joe & Marcy

Keith's laughter drew Jenny's attention from Joe's final words. "He just told me yesterday that we can't outgive God," he explained.

"I think the guy believes it," Jenny asserted and examined the seed until her eyes went misty. She looked up to find Keith staring at it too.

"This is a very special gift," Jenny said. "I don't know why it's affecting me like this, but I just feel something I can't quite explain."

"Yes, it's special, all right. It's God's message to us." Keith swallowed hard, and a spark of anticipation flashed through his dark eyes. "This could get exciting."

"Bring the whole tithe into the storehouse,
that there may be food in my house.
Test me in this," says the LORD Almighty,
"and see if I will not throw open the floodgates
of heaven and pour out so much blessing
that you will not have room enough for it."

MALACHI 3:10

Principle 1

When you are in a time of struggling and trials, take heart. Your soil is being tilled for the seed-planting time just around the corner.

Principle 2

Sow seed to meet your need.

Principle 3

Seed that is not planted is a crop that cannot grow. Always look for more ways to plant your money and talents, and your harvests will get larger and larger.

Principle 4

Even though you don't see evidence of growth, trust that your seed is taking root underground.

Principle 5

*Always use the best of the harvest as
seed for your next crop.*

Principle 6

You can't outgive God.

Principle 7

*If you want greater and more frequent harvests,
plant more seed more often.*

Principle 8

*Plan for the distribution of your harvest
when you plant the seed. Work in faith that the
harvest is coming.*

Principle 9

Always reserve seed for the next time of sowing.

Principle 10

*Harvesting takes teamwork. All share in the labor,
and all share in the rewards.*

DR. STAN A. TOLER is a general superintendent in the Church of the Nazarene with an office at the Global Ministry Center in Lenexa, Kansas, USA. He was chosen for the highest elected office in the church at the 27th General Assembly at Orlando, Florida, USA, in July 2009, after serving for 40 years as a pastor in Ohio, Florida, Tennessee, and Oklahoma. Stan Toler has written over 80 books, including his best-sellers, *God Has Never Failed Me, But He's Sure Scared Me to Death a Few Times*; *The Buzzards Are Circling, But God's Not Finished With Me Yet*; *God's Never Late, He's Seldom Early, He's Always Right on Time*; *The Secret Blend*; *Richest Person in the World*; *Practical Guide to Pastoral Ministry*; *The Inspirational Speaker's Resource*; *ReThink Your Life*; his popular *Minute Motivator* series, *If Only I Could Relate To The People I'm Related To* and his news book, *God Can Do Anything But Fail: So Try Para-Gliding in a Windstorm*. Toler for many years served as Vice-President and taught seminars for John C. Maxwell's INJOY Leadership Institute training church and corporate leaders to make a difference in the world. Recently, he was honored with a Doctorate of Divinity degree by Southern Nazarene University. He and his wife, Linda, an educator, have two married sons, Seth (Marcy) and Adam (Amanda), and two grandsons Rhett and Davis.

TO CONTACT THE AUTHOR

Stan Toler
E-mail: stan@stantoler.com
Website: www.StanToler.com

If you have enjoyed this book, or if it has impacted
your life, we would like to hear from you.

Please contact us at:
Dust Jacket Press
PO Box 721243
Oklahoma City, OK 73172

Or through our website: www.dustjacket.com